The Tale

The Tale

Joseph Conrad

ET REMOTISSIMA PROPE

Modern Voices

Modern Voices
Published by Hesperus Press Limited
4 Rickett Street, London SW6 1RU
www.hesperuspress.com

The Warrior's Soul first published in *Land & Water*, 1917
Prince Roman first published in *Oxford and Cambridge Review*, 1911
The Tale first published in *Strand Magazine*, 1917
The Black Mate first published in *London Magazine*, 1908

First published by Hesperus Press Limited, 2008

Foreword © Philip Hensher, 2008

Designed and typeset by Fraser Muggeridge studio
Printed in Jordan by the Jordan National Press

ISBN: 978-1-84391-444-0

Contents

Foreword

Conrad wrote massively without ever really writing on an expansive scale. His novels are never unusually long; the most substantial of them, *Nostromo*, is colossal only in its effects. Almost all his writing achieves the sense of the massive by savage abbreviation. The sense of catastrophe happening in full only elsewhere; the technique of bringing the reader up against a terrible fact which will be expanded on subsequently, as in *Chance* or *The Secret Agent*, or perhaps, as in 'Typhoon', only in the reader's imaginings; these are fundamental to Conrad's mature manner.

Most authors have a fictional length which somehow suits them, which seems the arena in which their gestures move most naturally. Dickens wrote best at 400,000 words; Chekhov at around 15,000. For a very successful author, the market will find ways to publish at his preferred length; the financially independent or reckless, such as Peacock or Firbank, will work at their natural length without thought of the consequences.

Conrad's most perfect and inspired productions are somewhere between the long short story, such as 'The Secret Sharer' and the short novel, such as *The Secret Agent*. In 'Typhoon' and *Heart of Darkness* you see him working at the sort of savagely abbreviated expansiveness which suits him most naturally. The greatness of the longer novels is the product of will and of exercised technique; the short stories proper have a peculiar, problematic magic which has eluded many of his most fervent admirers.

'The Tale' is one of his most horrible inventions, and almost everything is there. The curious erotic quality of the story's telling echoes *Chance* and 'The Secret Sharer'. The horrible act, carried out in the fluid and testing arena of the sea, can be paralleled a dozen times. There are powerful glimpses of the old virtuosity in natural description; here, the dense fog seems to be echoed in the syntactic evasions – 'I don't mean to say that the fog did not vary a little in its density'.

If 'The Tale' is a terrible distillation, 'The Black Mate' is a startling foreshadowing; one of Conrad's first stories, though not dug up and published until 1908. It doesn't take a literary historian to discern, in this genre exercise, some more personal preoccupations and favourite milieux beginning to surface. 'The Duel' is a more awkward story; the way the characters are attuned, Jamesianly, to each other's vibrations is frankly at odds with the romantic, historical setting.

Whether pouring the vast range of his interests into a pint-pot or trying to give some conventionally violent exchanges of the magazine short story a little refinement, Conrad's short stories are interesting, problematic, and always suggestive of their author's grand power. I suppose Conrad is my favourite novelist, though the word 'favourite' suggests an easier enjoyment than is really the case. The first piece of his writing I read, when I was fifteen or so, was 'The Secret Sharer'. Its world of hidden exchanges and unspoken, overheated eroticism expressed through a hushed act of storytelling was immediately alluring to me, though I found its intricate manner frankly difficult.

The odd thing is that the story has gone on being the object of absorbed fascination to me, and half a dozen other of Conrad's works – 'Typhoon', *The Secret Agent*, *Chance* and *Nostromo* above all – exert a gravitational pull. In part, the fascination is made up of those extraordinary sentences, where a not-quite right word takes on the power of great poetry – the 'dwarves, yelling with tiny throats' in *Nostromo*. In part, it is supplied by the massive climaxes of disenchantment and even bathos. The codas of 'Typhoon' and *Heart of Darkness* both bring romantic fury up against an indifferent listener, and the grandeur collapses in the sober light of the everyday, and of faint stupidity, scrupulously observed. That is the quality which makes me think of Conrad as one of the most adult of novelists, his structural dependence on disappointment and disenchantment.

But most of all, the fascination has to rest on Conrad's complex mastery of the arts of telling. Many of his best tales and novels are presented as stories told by a character in the course of what must, sometimes, have been very long evenings. Sometimes, as in *Chance*, these stories themselves contain shorter reported stories. It's worth noticing that the deeper into the layers of stories Conrad descends, the more intense the action often becomes.

And, so often, the most powerful moments in Conrad are, literally, twice-told tales. Very often, we know exactly what the conclusion is going to be, thanks to intricate doublings-back and repetitions, and, for some reason impossible to explain, the story, once the ending is in place and implacably unchangeable, becomes riveting. There is no stretch of fiction with the sinister pull of the second half of *The Secret Agent,* and there is no surprise in the conclusion at all.

Clearly, Conrad needed space to bring off these grand effects. His most characteristic effects, of doubling back and of burying a narrative deep in acts of telling, need a certain expansiveness to bring off, even if the final effect is usually one of brutal concision. When that brutal concision was forced on him by the requirements of the short story, the reader only has glimpses of his greatness. Where Kipling could be inspired by the requirements of brevity, you can feel Conrad either itching to expand beyond his limits, or working hard to fill it up.

Nevertheless, those glimpses of greatness are still greatness; and the cruel chill of 'The Tale' and the frank enjoyment of the horrid in 'The Black Mate' are authentic enough. Conrad is a writer who must be read in his entirety, and there is not a page of his without a little spasm of his anguished, serious, adult spirit.

– Philip Hensher, 2008

The Tale

The Warrior's Soul

The old officer with long white moustaches gave rein to his indignation.

'Is it possible that you youngsters should have no more sense than that! Some of you had better wipe the milk off your upper lip before you start to pass judgment on the few poor stragglers of a generation which has done and suffered not a little in its time.'

His hearers having expressed much compunction the ancient warrior became appeased. But he was not silenced.

'I am one of them – one of the stragglers, I mean,' he went on patiently. 'And what did we do? What have we achieved? He – the great Napoleon – started upon us to emulate the Macedonian Alexander, with a ruck of nations at his back. We opposed empty spaces to French impetuosity, then we offered them an interminable battle so that their army went at last to sleep in its positions lying down on the heaps of its own dead. Then came the wall of fire in Moscow. It toppled down on them.

'Then began the long rout of the Grand Army. I have seen it stream on, like the doomed flight of haggard, spectral sinners across the innermost frozen circle of Dante's *Inferno*, ever widening before their despairing eyes.

'They who escaped must have had their souls doubly riveted inside their bodies to carry them out of Russia through that frost fit to split rocks. But to say that it was our fault that a single one of them got away is mere ignorance. Why! Our own men suffered nearly to the limit of their strength. Their Russian strength!

'Of course our spirit was not broken; and then our cause was good – it was holy. But that did not temper the wind much to men and horses.

'The flesh is weak. Good or evil purpose, Humanity has to pay the price. Why! In that very fight for that little village of which I have been telling you we were fighting for the shelter of those old houses as much as victory. And with the French it was the same.

'It wasn't for the sake of glory, or for the sake of strategy. The French knew that they would have to retreat before morning and we knew perfectly well that they would go. As far as the war was concerned there was nothing to fight about. Yet our infantry and theirs fought like wild cats, or like heroes if you like that better, amongst the houses – hot work enough – while the supports out in the open stood freezing in a tempestuous north wind which drove the snow on earth and the great masses of clouds in the sky at a terrific pace. The very air was inexpressibly sombre by contrast with the white earth. I have never seen God's creation look more sinister than on that day.

'We, the cavalry (we were only a handful), had not much to do except turn our backs to the wind and receive some stray French round shot. This, I may tell you, was the last of the French guns and it was the last time they had their artillery in position. Those guns never went away from there either. We found them abandoned next morning. But that afternoon they were keeping up an infernal fire on our attacking column; the furious wind carried away the smoke and even the noise but we could see the constant flicker of the tongues of fire along the French front. Then a driving flurry of snow would hide everything except the dark red flashes in the white swirl.

'At intervals when the line cleared we could see away across the plain to the right a sombre column moving endlessly; the great rout of the Grand Army creeping on and on all the time while the fight on our left went on with a great din and fury. The cruel whirlwind of snow swept over that scene of death and desolation. And then the wind fell as suddenly as it had arisen in the morning.

'Presently we got orders to charge the retreating column; I don't know why unless they wanted to prevent us from getting frozen in our saddles by giving us something to do. We changed front half right and got into motion at a walk to take that distant dark line in flank. It might have been half past two in the afternoon.

'You must know that so far in this campaign my regiment had never been on the main line of Napoleon's advance. All these months since the invasion the army we belonged to had been wrestling with Oudinot in the north. We had only come down lately, driving him before us to the Beresina.

'This was the first occasion, then, that I and my comrades had a close view of Napoleon's Grand Army. It was an amazing and terrible sight. I had heard of it from others; I had seen the stragglers from it: small bands of marauders, parties of prisoners in the distance. But this was the very column itself! A crawling, stumbling, starved, half-demented mob. It issued from the forest a mile away and its head was lost in the murk of the fields. We rode into it at a trot, which was the most we could get out of our horses, and we stuck in that human mass as if in a moving bog. There was no resistance. I heard a few shots, half a dozen perhaps. Their very senses seemed frozen within them. I had time for a good look while riding at the head of my squadron. Well, I assure you, there were men walking on the outer edge so lost to everything but their misery that they never turned their heads to look at our charge. Soldiers!

'My horse pushed over one of them with his chest. The poor wretch had a dragoon's blue cloak, all torn and scorched, hanging from his shoulders and he didn't even put his hand out to snatch at my bridle and save himself. He just went down.

Our troopers were pointing and slashing; well, and of course at first I myself... What would you have! An enemy's an enemy. Yet a sort of sickening awe crept into my heart. There was no tumult – only a low deep murmur dwelt over them interspersed with louder cries and groans while that mob kept on pushing and surging past us, sightless and without feeling. A smell of scorched rags and festering wounds hung in the air. My horse staggered in the eddies of swaying men. But it was like cutting down galvanised corpses that didn't care. Invaders! Yes... God was already dealing with them.

'I touched my horse with the spurs to get clear. There was a sudden rush and a sort of angry moan when our second squadron got into them on our right. My horse plunged and somebody got hold of my leg. As I had no mind to get pulled out of the saddle I gave a backhanded slash without looking. I heard a cry and my leg was let go suddenly.

'Just then I caught sight of the subaltern of my troop at some little distance from me. His name was Tomassov. That multitude of resurrected bodies with glassy eyes was seething round his horse as if blind, growling crazily. He was sitting erect in his saddle, not looking down at them and sheathing his sword deliberately.

'This Tomassov, well, he had a beard. Of course we all had beards then. Circumstances, lack of leisure, want of razors, too. No, seriously, we were a wild-looking lot in those unforgotten days which so many, so very many of us did not survive. You know our losses were awful, too. Yes, we looked wild. *Des Russes sauvages* – what!

'So he had a beard – this Tomassov I mean; but he did not look *sauvage*. He was the youngest of us all. And that meant real youth. At a distance he passed muster fairly well, what with the grime and the particular stamp of that campaign on our faces. But directly you were near enough to have a good look into his eyes, that was where his lack of age showed, though he was not exactly a boy.

'Those same eyes were blue, something like the blue of autumn skies, dreamy and gay, too – innocent, believing eyes. A topknot of fair hair decorated his brow like a gold diadem in what one would call normal times.

'You may think I am talking of him as if he were the hero of a novel. Why, that's nothing to what the adjutant discovered about him. He discovered that he had a "lover's lips" – whatever that may be. If the adjutant meant a nice mouth, why, it was nice enough, but of course it was intended for a sneer. That adjutant of ours was not a very delicate fellow. "Look at those lover's lips," he would exclaim in a loud tone while Tomassov was talking.

'Tomassov didn't quite like that sort of thing. But to a certain extent he had laid himself open to banter by the lasting character of his impressions which were connected with the passion of love and, perhaps, were not of such a rare kind as he seemed to think them. What made his comrades tolerant of his rhapsodies was the fact that they were connected with France, with Paris!

'You of the present generation, you cannot conceive how much prestige there was then in those names for the whole world. Paris was the centre of wonder for all human beings gifted with imagination. There we were, the majority of us young and well connected, but not long out of our hereditary nests in the provinces; simple servants of God; mere rustics, if I may say so. So we were only too ready to listen to the tales of France from our comrade Tomassov. He had been attached to our mission in Paris the year before the war. High protections very likely – or maybe sheer luck.

'I don't think he could have been a very useful member of the mission because of his youth and complete inexperience. And apparently all his time in Paris was his own. The use he made of it was to fall in love, to remain in that state, to cultivate it, to exist only for it in a manner of speaking.

'Thus it was something more than a mere memory that he had brought with him from France. Memory is a fugitive thing. It can be falsified, it can be effaced, it can be even doubted. Why! I myself come to doubt sometimes that I, too, have been in Paris in my turn. And the long road there with battles for its stages would appear still more incredible if it were not for a certain musket ball which I have been carrying about my person ever since a little cavalry affair which happened in Silesia at the very beginning of the Leipzig campaign.

'Passages of love, however, are more impressive perhaps than passages of danger. You don't go affronting love in troops as it were. They are rarer, more personal and more intimate. And remember that with Tomassov all that was very fresh yet. He had not been home from France three months when the war began.

'His heart, his mind were full of that experience. He was really awed by it, and he was simple enough to let it appear in his speeches. He considered himself a sort of privileged person, not because a woman had looked at him with favour, but simply because, how shall I say it, he had had the wonderful illumination of his worship for her, as if it were heaven itself that had done this for him.

'Oh yes, he was very simple. A nice youngster, yet no fool; and with that, utterly inexperienced, unsuspicious, and un-thinking. You will find one like that here and there in the provinces. He had some poetry in him too. It could only be natural, something quite his own, not acquired. I suppose Father Adam had some poetry in him of that natural sort. For the rest *un Russe sauvage* as the French sometimes call us, but not of that kind which, they maintain, eats tallow candle for a delicacy.

As to the woman, the French woman, well, though I have also been in France with a hundred thousand Russians, I have never seen her. Very likely she was not in Paris then. And in any case hers were not the doors that would fly open before simple fellows of my sort, you understand. Gilded salons were never in my way. I could not tell you how she looked, which is strange considering that I was, if I may say so, Tomassov's special confidant.

'He very soon got shy of talking before the others. I suppose the usual campfire comments jarred his fine feelings. But I was left to him and truly I had to submit. You can't very well expect a youngster in Tomassov's state to hold his tongue altogether; and I – I suppose you will hardly believe me – I am by nature a rather silent sort of person.

'Very likely my silence appeared to him sympathetic. All the month of September our regiment, quartered in villages, had come in for an easy time. It was then that I heard most of that – you can't call it a story. The story I have in my mind is not in that. Outpourings, let us call them.

'I would sit quite content to hold my peace, a whole hour perhaps, while Tomassov talked with exaltation. And when he was done I would still hold my peace. And then there would be produced a solemn effect of silence which, I imagine, pleased Tomassov in a way.

'She was of course not a woman in her first youth. A widow, maybe. At any rate I never heard Tomassov mention her husband. She had a salon, something very distinguished; a social centre in which she queened it with great splendour.

'Somehow, I fancy her court was composed mostly of men. But Tomassov, I must say, kept such details out of his discourses wonderfully well. Upon my word I don't know whether her hair was dark or fair, her eyes brown or blue; what was her stature, her features, or her complexion. His love soared above mere physical impressions. He never described her to me in set terms;

but he was ready to swear that in her presence everybody's thoughts and feelings were bound to circle round her. She was that sort of woman. Most wonderful conversations on all sorts of subjects went on in her salon: but through them all there flowed unheard like a mysterious strain of music the assertion, the power, the tyranny of sheer beauty. So apparently the woman was beautiful. She detached all these talking people from their life interests, and even from their vanities. She was a secret delight and a secret trouble. All the men when they looked at her fell to brooding as if struck by the thought that their lives had been wasted. She was the very joy and shudder of felicity and she brought only sadness and torment to the hearts of men.

'In short, she must have been an extraordinary woman, or else Tomassov was an extraordinary young fellow to feel in that way and to talk like this about her. I told you the fellow had a lot of poetry in him and observed that all this sounded true enough. It would be just about the sorcery a woman very much out of the common would exercise, you know. Poets do get close to truth somehow – there is no denying that.

'There is no poetry in my composition, I know, but I have my share of common shrewdness, and I have no doubt that the lady was kind to the youngster, once he did find his way inside her salon. His getting in is the real marvel. However, he did get in, the innocent, and he found himself in distinguished company there, amongst men of considerable position. And you know, what that means: thick waists, bald heads, teeth that are not – as some satirist puts it. Imagine amongst them a nice boy, fresh and simple, like an apple just off the tree; a modest, good-looking, impressionable, adoring young barbarian. My word! What a change! What a relief for jaded feelings! And with that, having in his nature that dose of poetry which saves even a simpleton from being a fool.

'He became an artlessly, unconditionally devoted slave. He was rewarded by being smiled on and in time admitted to the intimacy of the house. It may be that the unsophisticated young barbarian amused the exquisite lady. Perhaps – since he didn't feed on tallow candles – he satisfied some need of tenderness in the woman. You know, there are many kinds of tenderness highly civilised women are capable of. Women with heads and imagination, I mean, and no temperament to speak of, you understand. But who is going to fathom their needs or their fancies? Most of the time they themselves don't know much about their innermost moods, and blunder out of one into another, sometimes with catastrophic results. And then who is more surprised than they? However, Tomassov's case was in its nature quite idyllic. The fashionable world was amused. His devotion made for him a kind of social success. But he didn't care. There was his one divinity, and there was the shrine where he was permitted to go in and out without regard for official reception hours.

'He took advantage of that privilege freely. Well, he had no official duties, you know. The Military Mission was supposed to be more complimentary than anything else, the head of it being a personal friend of our Emperor Alexander; and he, too, was laying himself out for successes in fashionable life exclusively – as it seemed. As it seemed.

'One afternoon Tomassov called on the mistress of his thoughts earlier than usual. She was not alone. There was a man with her, not one of the thick-waisted, bald-headed personages, but a somebody all the same, a man over thirty, a French officer who to some extent was also a privileged intimate. Tomassov was not jealous of him. Such a sentiment would have appeared presumptuous to the simple fellow.

'On the contrary he admired that officer. You have no idea of the French military men's prestige in those days, even with us Russian soldiers who had managed to face them perhaps better than the rest. Victory had marked them on the forehead – it seemed forever. They would have been more than human if they had not been conscious of it; but they were good comrades and had a sort of brotherly feeling for all who bore arms, even if it was against them.

'And this was quite a superior example, an officer of the major-general's staff, and a man of the best society besides. He was powerfully built, and thoroughly masculine, though he was as carefully groomed as a woman. He had the courteous self-possession of a man of the world. His forehead, white as alabaster, contrasted impressively with the healthy colour of his face.

'I don't know whether he was jealous of Tomassov, but I suspect that he might have been a little annoyed at him as at a sort of walking absurdity of the sentimental order. But these men of the world are impenetrable, and outwardly he condescended to recognise Tomassov's existence even more distinctly than was strictly necessary. Once or twice he had offered him some useful worldly advice with perfect tact and delicacy. Tomassov was completely conquered by that evidence of kindness under the cold polish of the best society.

'Tomassov, introduced into the *petit salon*, found these two exquisite people sitting on a sofa together and had the feeling of having interrupted some special conversation. They looked at him strangely, he thought; but he was not given to understand that he had intruded. After a time the lady said to the officer – his name was De Castel – "I wish you would take the trouble to ascertain the exact truth as to that rumour."

'"It's much more than a mere rumour," remarked the officer. But he got up submissively and went out. The lady turned to Tomassov and said, "You may stay with me."

'This express command made him supremely happy, though as a matter of fact he had had no idea of going.

'She regarded him with her kindly glances, which made something glow and expand within his chest. It was a delicious feeling, even though it did cut one's breath short now and then. Ecstatically he drank in the sound of her tranquil, seductive talk full of innocent gaiety and of spiritual quietude. His passion appeared to him to flame up and envelop her in blue fiery tongues from head to foot and over her head, while her soul reposed in the centre like a big white rose...

'H'm, good this. He told me many other things like that. But this is the one I remember. He himself remembered everything because these were the last memories of that woman. He was seeing her for the last time though he did not know it then.

'M. De Castel returned, breaking into that atmosphere of enchantment Tomassov had been drinking in even to complete unconsciousness of the external world. Tomassov could not help being struck by the distinction of his movements, the ease of his manner, his superiority to all the other men he knew, and he suffered from it. It occurred to him that these two brilliant beings on the sofa were made for each other.

'De Castel sitting down by the side of the lady murmured to her discreetly, "There is not the slightest doubt that it's true," and they both turned their eyes to Tomassov. Roused thoroughly from his enchantment he became self-conscious; a feeling of shyness came over him. He sat smiling faintly at them.

'The lady without taking her eyes off the blushing Tomassov said with a dreamy gravity quite unusual to her:

'"I should like to know that your generosity can be supreme – without a flaw. Love at its highest should be the origin of every perfection."

'Tomassov opened his eyes wide with admiration at this, as though her lips had been dropping real pearls. The sentiment, however, was not uttered for the primitive Russian youth but for the exquisitely accomplished man of the world, De Castel.

'Tomassov could not see the effect it produced because the French officer lowered his head and sat there contemplating his admirably polished boots. The lady whispered in a sympathetic tone:

'"You have scruples?"

'De Castel, without looking up, murmured, "It could be turned into a nice point of honour."

'She said vivaciously, "That surely is artificial. I am all for natural feelings. I believe in nothing else. But perhaps your conscience…"

'He interrupted her, "Not at all. My conscience is not childish. The fate of those people is of no military importance to us. What can it matter? The fortune of France is invincible."

'"Well then…" she uttered, meaningly, and rose from the couch. The French officer stood up, too. Tomassov hastened to follow their example. He was pained by his state of utter mental darkness. While he was raising the lady's white hand to his lips he heard the French officer say with marked emphasis:

'"If he has the soul of a warrior," (at that time, you know, people really talked in that way), "if he has the soul of a warrior he ought to fall at your feet in gratitude."

'Tomassov felt himself plunged into even denser darkness than before. He followed the French officer out of the room and out of the house; for he had a notion that this was expected of him.

'It was getting dusk, the weather was very bad, and the street was quite deserted. The Frenchman lingered in it strangely. And Tomassov lingered, too, without impatience. He was never in a hurry to get away from the house in which she lived. And besides, something wonderful had happened to him. The hand he had reverently raised by the tips of its fingers had been pressed against his lips. He had received a secret favour! He was almost frightened. The world had reeled – and it had hardly steadied itself yet. De Castel stopped short at the corner of the quiet street.

'"I don't care to be seen too much with you in the lighted thoroughfares, M. Tomassov," he said in a strangely grim tone.

'"Why?" asked the young man, too startled to be offended.

'"From prudence," answered the other curtly. "So we will have to part here; but before we part I'll disclose to you something of which you will see at once the importance."

'This, please note, was an evening in late March of the year 1812. For a long time already there had been talk of a growing coolness between Russia and France. The word war was being whispered in drawing rooms louder and louder, and at last was heard in official circles. Thereupon the Parisian police discovered that our military envoy had corrupted some clerks at the Ministry of War and had obtained from them some very important confidential documents. The wretched men (there were two of them) had confessed their crime and were to be shot that night. Tomorrow all the town would be talking of the affair. But the worst was that the Emperor Napoleon was furiously angry at the discovery, and had made up his mind to have the Russian envoy arrested.

'Such was De Castel's disclosure; and though he had spoken in low tones Tomassov was stunned as by a great crash.

'"Arrested," he murmured, desolately.

'"Yes, and kept as a state prisoner – with everybody belonging to him…"

'The French officer seized Tomassov's arm above the elbow and pressed it hard.

'"And kept in France," he repeated into Tomassov's very ear, and then letting him go stepped back a space and remained silent.

'"And it's you, you, who are telling me this!" cried Tomassov in an extremity of gratitude that was hardly greater than his admiration for the generosity of his future foe. Could a brother have done for him more! He sought to seize the hand of the French officer, but the latter remained wrapped up closely in his cloak. Possibly in the dark he had not noticed the attempt. He moved back a bit and in his self-possessed voice of a man of the world, as though he were speaking across a card table or something of the sort, he called Tomassov's attention to the fact that if he meant to make use of the warning the moments were precious.

'"Indeed they are," agreed the awed Tomassov. "Goodbye then. I have no word of thanks to equal your generosity; but if ever I have an opportunity, I swear it, you may command my life…"

'But the Frenchman retreated, had already vanished in the dark lonely street. Tomassov was alone, and then he did not waste any of the precious minutes of that night.

'See how people's mere gossip and idle talk pass into history. In all the memoirs of the time if you read them you will find it stated that our envoy had a warning from some highly placed woman who was in love with him. Of course it's known that he had successes with women, and in the highest spheres, too, but the truth is that the person who warned him was no other than our simple Tomassov – an altogether different sort of lover from himself.

'This then is the secret of our Emperor's representative's escape from arrest. He and all his official household got out of France all right – as history records.

'And amongst that household there was our Tomassov of course. He had, in the words of the French officer, the soul of a warrior. And what more desolate prospect for a man with such a soul than to be imprisoned on the eve of war; to be cut off from his country in danger, from his military family, from his duty, from honour, and – well – from glory, too.

'Tomassov used to shudder at the mere thought of the moral torture he had escaped; and he nursed in his heart a boundless gratitude to the two people who had saved him from that cruel ordeal. They were wonderful! For him love and friendship were but two aspects of exalted perfection. He had found these fine examples of it and he vowed them indeed a sort of cult. It affected his attitude towards Frenchmen in general, great patriot as he was. He was naturally indignant at the invasion of his country, but this indignation had no personal animosity in it. His was fundamentally a fine nature. He grieved at the appalling amount of human suffering he saw around him. Yes, he was full of compassion for all forms of mankind's misery in a manly way.

'Less fine natures than his own did not understand this very well. In the regiment they had nicknamed him the Humane Tomassov.

'He didn't take offence at it. There is nothing incompatible between humanity and a warrior's soul. People without compassion are the civilians, government officials, merchants and such like. As to the ferocious talk one hears from a lot of decent people in war time – well, the tongue is an unruly member at best and when there is some excitement going on there is no curbing its furious activity.

'So I had not been very surprised to see our Tomassov sheathe deliberately his sword right in the middle of that charge, you may say. As we rode away after it he was very silent. He was not a chatterer as a rule, but it was evident that this close view of the Grand Army had affected him deeply, like some sight not of this earth. I had always been a pretty tough individual myself – well, even I... and there was that fellow with a lot of poetry in his nature! You may imagine what he made of it to himself. We rode side by side without opening our lips. It was simply beyond words.

'We established our bivouac along the edge of the forest so as to get some shelter for our horses. However, the boisterous north wind had dropped as quickly as it had sprung up, and the great winter stillness lay on the land from the Baltic to the Black Sea. One could almost feel its cold, lifeless immensity reaching up to the stars.

'Our men had lighted several fires for their officers and had cleared the snow around them. We had big logs of wood for seats; it was a very tolerable bivouac upon the whole, even without the exultation of victory. We were to feel that later, but at present we were oppressed by our stern and arduous task.

'There were three of us round my fire. The third one was that adjutant. He was perhaps a well-meaning chap but not so nice as he might have been had he been less rough in manner and less crude in his perceptions. He would reason about people's conduct as though a man were as simple a figure as, say, two sticks laid across each other; whereas a man is much more like the sea whose movements are too complicated to explain, and whose depths may bring up God only knows what at any moment.

'We talked a little about that charge. Not much. That sort of thing does not lend itself to conversation. Tomassov muttered a few words about a mere butchery. I had nothing to say. As I told you I had very soon let my sword hang idle at my wrist. That starving mob had not even *tried* to defend itself. Just a few shots. We had two men wounded. Two!... and we had charged the main column of Napoleon's Grand Army.

'Tomassov muttered wearily, "What was the good of it?" I did not wish to argue, so I only just mumbled, "Ah, well!" But the adjutant struck in unpleasantly:

'"Why, it warmed the men a bit. It has made me warm. That's a good enough reason. But our Tomassov is so humane! And besides he has been in love with a French woman, and thick as thieves with a lot of Frenchmen, so he is sorry for them. Never mind, my boy, we are on the Paris road now and you shall soon see her!" This was one of his usual, as we believed them, foolish speeches. None of us but believed that the getting to Paris would be a matter of years – of years. And lo! less than eighteen months afterwards I was rooked of a lot of money in a gambling hell in the Palais Royal.

'Truth, being often the most senseless thing in the world, is sometimes revealed to fools. I don't think that adjutant of ours believed in his own words. He just wanted to tease Tomassov from habit. Purely from habit. We of course said nothing, and so he took his head in his hands and fell into a doze as he sat on a log in front of the fire.

'Our cavalry was on the extreme right wing of the army, and I must confess that we guarded it very badly. We had lost all sense of insecurity by this time; but still we did keep up a pretence of doing it in a way. Presently a trooper rode up leading a horse and Tomassov mounted stiffly and went off on a round of the outposts. Of the perfectly useless outposts.

'The night was still, except for the crackling of the fires. The raging wind had lifted far above the earth and not the faintest breath of it could be heard. Only the full moon swam out with a rush into the sky and suddenly hung high and motionless overhead. I remember raising my hairy face to it for a moment. Then, I verily believe, I dozed off, too, bent double on my log with my head towards the fierce blaze.

'You know what an impermanent thing such slumber is. One moment you drop into an abyss and the next you are back in the world that you would think too deep for any noise but the trumpet of the Last Judgment. And then off you go again. Your very soul seems to slip down into a bottomless black pit. Then up once more into a startled consciousness. A mere plaything of cruel sleep one is, then. Tormented both ways.

'However, when my orderly appeared before me, repeating, "Won't your Honour be pleased to eat?… Won't your Honour be pleased to eat?…" I managed to keep my hold of it – I mean that gaping consciousness. He was offering me a sooty pot containing some grain boiled in water with a pinch of salt. A wooden spoon was stuck in it.

'At that time these were the only rations we were getting regularly. Mere chicken food, confound it! But the Russian soldier is wonderful. Well, my fellow waited till I had feasted and then went away carrying off the empty pot.

'I was no longer sleepy. Indeed, I had become awake with an exaggerated mental consciousness of existence extending beyond my immediate surroundings. Those are but exceptional moments with mankind, I am glad to say. I had the intimate sensation of the earth in all its enormous expanse wrapped in snow, with nothing showing on it but trees with their straight stalk-like trunks and their funeral verdure; and in this aspect of general mourning I seemed to hear the sighs of mankind falling to die in the midst of a nature without life. They were French-men. We didn't hate them; they did not hate us; we had existed far apart – and suddenly they had come rolling in with arms in their hands, without fear of God, carrying with them other nations, and all to perish together in a long, long trail of frozen corpses. I had an actual vision of that trail: a pathetic multitude of small dark mounds stretching away under the moonlight in a clear, still, and pitiless atmosphere – a sort of horrible peace.

'But what other peace could there be for them? What else did they deserve? I don't know by what connection of emotions there came into my head the thought that the earth was a pagan planet and not a fit abode for Christian virtues.

'You may be surprised that I should remember all this so well. What is a passing emotion or half-formed thought to last in so many years of a man's changing, inconsequential life? But what has fixed the emotion of that evening in my recollection so that the slightest shadows remain indelible was an event of strange finality, an event not likely to be forgotten in a lifetime – as you shall see.

'I don't suppose I had been entertaining those thoughts more than five minutes when something induced me to look over my shoulder. I can't think it was a noise; the snow deadened all the sounds. Something it must have been, some sort of signal reaching my consciousness. Anyway, I turned my head, and there was the event approaching me, not that I knew it or had the slightest premonition. All I saw in the distance were two figures approaching in the moonlight. One of them was our Tomassov. The dark mass behind him which moved across my sight were the horses which his orderly was leading away. Tomassov was a very familiar appearance, in long boots, a tall figure ending in a pointed hood. But by his side advanced another figure. I mistrusted my eyes at first. It was amazing! It had a shining crested helmet on its head and was muffled up in a white cloak. The cloak was not as white as snow. Nothing in the world is. It was white more like mist, with an aspect that was ghostly and martial to an extraordinary degree. It was as if Tomassov had got hold of the God of War himself. I could see at once that he was leading this resplendent vision by the arm. Then I saw that he was holding it up. While I stared and stared, they crept on – for indeed they were creeping – and at last they crept into the light of our bivouac fire and passed beyond the log I was sitting on. The blaze played on the helmet. It was extremely battered and the frostbitten face, full of sores, under it was framed in bits of mangy fur. No God of War this, but a French officer. The great white cuirassier's cloak was torn, burnt full of holes. His feet were wrapped up in old sheepskins over remnants of boots. They looked monstrous and he tottered on them, sustained by Tomassov who lowered him most carefully on to the log on which I sat.

'My amazement knew no bounds.

'"You have brought in a prisoner," I said to Tomassov, as if I could not believe my eyes.

'You must understand that unless they surrendered in large bodies we made no prisoners. What would have been the good? Our Cossacks either killed the stragglers or else let them alone, just as it happened. It came really to the same thing in the end.

'Tomassov turned to me with a very troubled look.

'"He sprang up from the ground somewhere as I was leaving the outpost," he said. "I believe he was making for it, for he walked blindly into my horse. He got hold of my leg and of course none of our chaps dared touch him then."

'"He had a narrow escape," I said.

'"He didn't appreciate it," said Tomassov, looking even more troubled than before. "He came along holding to my stirrup leather. That's what made me so late. He told me he was a staff officer; and then talking in a voice such, I suppose, as the damned alone use, a croaking of rage and pain, he said he had a favour to beg of me. A supreme favour. Did I understand him, he asked in a sort of fiendish whisper.

'"Of course I told him that I did. I said, '*oui, je vous comprends.*'

'"Then," said he, "do it. Now! At once – in the pity of your heart."

'Tomassov ceased and stared queerly at me above the head of the prisoner.

'I said, "What did he mean?"

'"That's what I asked him," answered Tomassov in a dazed tone, "and he said that he wanted me to do him the favour to blow his brains out. As a fellow soldier he said. "As a man of feeling – as – as a humane man."

'The prisoner sat between us like an awful gashed mummy as to the face, a martial scarecrow, a grotesque horror of rags and dirt, with awful living eyes, full of vitality, full of unquenchable fire, in a body of horrible affliction, a skeleton at the feast of glory. And suddenly those shining unextinguishable eyes of his became fixed upon Tomassov. He, poor fellow, fascinated, returned the ghastly stare of a suffering soul in that mere husk of a man. The prisoner croaked at him in French.

'"I recognise you now. You are her Russian youngster. You were very grateful. I call on you to pay the debt. Pay it, I say, with one liberating shot. You are a man of honour. I have not even a broken sabre. All my being recoils from my own degradation. You know me."

'Tomassov said nothing.

'"Haven't you got the soul of a warrior?" the Frenchman asked in an angry whisper, but with something of a mocking intention in it.

'"I don't know," said poor Tomassov.

'What a look of contempt that scarecrow gave him out of his unquenchable eyes. He seemed to live only by the force of infuriated and impotent despair. Suddenly he gave a gasp and fell forward writhing in the agony of cramp in all his limbs; a not unusual effect of the heat of a campfire. It resembled the application of some horrible torture. But he tried to fight against the pain at first. He only moaned low while we bent over him so as to prevent him rolling into the fire, and muttered feverishly at intervals, "*Tuez moi, tuez moi...*" till, vanquished by the pain, he screamed in agony, time after time, each cry bursting out through his compressed lips.

'The adjutant woke up on the other side of the fire and started swearing awfully at the beastly row that Frenchman was making.

'"What's this? More of your infernal humanity, Tomassov," he yelled at us. "Why don't you have him thrown out of this to the devil on the snow?"

'As we paid no attention to his shouts, he got up, cursing shockingly, and went away to another fire. Presently the French officer became easier. We propped him up against the log and sat silent on each side of him till the bugles started their call at the first break of day. The big flame, kept up all through the night, paled on the livid sheet of snow, while the frozen air all round rang with the brazen notes of cavalry trumpets. The Frenchman's eyes, fixed in a glassy stare, which for a moment made us hope that he had died quietly sitting there between us two, stirred slowly to right and left, looking at each of our faces in turn. Tomassov and I exchanged glances of dismay. Then De Castel's voice, unexpected in its renewed strength and ghastly self-possession, made us shudder inwardly.

'"*Bonjour, Messieurs.*"

'His chin dropped on his breast. Tomassov addressed me in Russian.

'"It is he, the man himself…" I nodded and Tomassov went on in a tone of anguish, "Yes, he! Brilliant, accomplished, envied by men, loved by that woman – this horror – this miserable thing that cannot die. Look at his eyes. It's terrible."

'I did not look, but I understood what Tomassov meant. We could do nothing for him. This avenging winter of fate held both the fugitives and the pursuers in its iron grip. Compassion was but a vain word before that unrelenting destiny. I tried to say something about a convoy being no doubt collected in the village – but I faltered at the mute glance Tomassov gave me. We knew what those convoys were like: appalling mobs of hopeless wretches driven on by the butts of Cossacks' lances, back to the frozen inferno, with their faces set away from their homes.

'Our two squadrons had been formed along the edge of the forest. The minutes of anguish were passing. The Frenchman suddenly struggled to his feet. We helped him almost without knowing what we were doing.

'"Come," he said, in measured tones. "This is the moment."
He paused for a long time, then with the same distinctness went
on: "On my word of honour, all faith is dead in me."

'His voice lost suddenly its self-possession. After waiting
a little while he added in a murmur, "And even my courage…
Upon my honour."

'Another long pause ensued before, with a great effort, he
whispered hoarsely, "Isn't this enough to move a heart of stone?
Am I to go on my knees to you?"

'Again a deep silence fell upon the three of us. Then the
French officer flung his last word of anger at Tomassov.

'"Milksop!"

'Not a feature of the poor fellow moved. I made up my mind
to go and fetch a couple of our troopers to lead that miserable
prisoner away to the village. There was nothing else for it. I had
not moved six paces towards the group of horses and orderlies
in front of our squadron when… but you have guessed it. Of
course. And I, too, I guessed it, for I give you my word that the
report of Tomassov's pistol was the most insignificant thing
imaginable. The snow certainly does absorb sound. It was a mere
feeble pop. Of the orderlies holding our horses I don't think one
turned his head round.

'Yes. Tomassov had done it. Destiny had led that De Castel
to the man who could understand him perfectly. But it was
poor Tomassov's lot to be the predestined victim. You know
what the world's justice and mankind's judgment are like. They
fell heavily on him with a sort of inverted hypocrisy. Why! That
brute of an adjutant, himself, was the first to set going horrified
allusions to the shooting of a prisoner in cold blood! Tomassov
was not dismissed from the service of course. But after the siege
of Danzig he asked for permission to resign from the army, and
went away to bury himself in the depths of his province, where
a vague story of some dark deed clung to him for years.

'Yes. He had done it. And what was it? One warrior's soul paying its debt a hundredfold to another warrior's soul by releasing it from a fate worse than death – the loss of all faith and courage. You may look on it in that way. I don't know. And perhaps poor Tomassov did not know himself. But I was the first to approach that appalling dark group on the snow: the Frenchman extended rigidly on his back, Tomassov kneeling on one knee rather nearer to the feet than to the Frenchman's head. He had taken his cap off and his hair shone like gold in the light drift of flakes that had begun to fall. He was stooping over the dead in a tenderly contemplative attitude. And his young, ingenuous face, with lowered eyelids, expressed no grief, no sternness, no horror – but was set in the repose of a profound, as if endless and endlessly silent, meditation.'

Prince Roman

'Events which happened seventy years ago are perhaps rather too far off to be dragged aptly into a mere conversation. Of course the year 1831 is for us an historical date, one of these fatal years when in the presence of the world's passive indignation and eloquent sympathies we had once more to murmur "*Vo Victis*" and count the cost in sorrow. Not that we were ever very good at calculating, either, in prosperity or in adversity. That's a lesson we could never learn, to the great exasperation of our enemies who have bestowed upon us the epithet of Incorrigible...'

The speaker was of Polish nationality, that nationality not so much alive as surviving, which persists in thinking, breathing, speaking, hoping, and suffering in its grave, railed in by a million of bayonets and triple-sealed with the seals of three great empires.

The conversation was about aristocracy. How did this, nowadays discredited, subject come up? It is some years ago now and the precise recollection has faded. But I remember that it was not considered practically as an ingredient in the social mixture; and I verily believed that we arrived at that subject through some exchange of ideas about patriotism – a somewhat discredited sentiment, because the delicacy of our humanitarians regards it as a relic of barbarism. Yet neither the great Florentine painter who closed his eyes in death thinking of his city, nor St Francis blessing with his last breath the town of Assisi, were barbarians. It requires a certain greatness of soul to interpret patriotism worthily – or else a sincerity of feeling denied to the vulgar refinement of modern thought which cannot understand the august simplicity of a sentiment proceeding from the very nature of things and men.

The aristocracy we were talking about was the very highest, the great families of Europe, not impoverished, not converted, not liberalised, the most distinctive and specialised class of all classes, for which even ambition itself does not exist among the usual incentives to activity and regulators of conduct.

The undisputed right of leadership having passed away from them, we judged that their great fortunes, their cosmopolitanism brought about by wide alliances, their elevated station, in which there is so little to gain and so much to lose, must make their position difficult in times of political commotion or national upheaval. No longer born to command – which is the very essence of aristocracy – it becomes difficult for them to do aught else but hold aloof from the great movements of popular passion.

We had reached that conclusion when the remark about far-off events was made and the date of 1831 mentioned. And the speaker continued:

'I don't mean to say that I knew Prince Roman at that remote time. I begin to feel pretty ancient, but I am not so ancient as that. In fact Prince Roman was married the very year my father was born. It was in 1828; the 19th century was young yet and the Prince was even younger than the century, but I don't know exactly by how much. In any case his was an early marriage. It was an ideal alliance from every point of view. The girl was young and beautiful, an orphan heiress of a great name and of a great fortune. The Prince, then an officer in the Guards and distinguished amongst his fellows by something reserved and reflective in his character, had fallen headlong in love with her beauty, her charm, and the serious qualities of her mind and heart. He was a rather silent young man; but his glances, his bearing, his whole person expressed his absolute devotion to the woman of his choice, a devotion which she returned in her own frank and fascinating manner.

'The flame of this pure young passion promised to burn forever; and for a season it lit up the dry, cynical atmosphere of the great world of St Petersburg. The Emperor Nicholas himself, the grandfather of the present man, the one who died from the Crimean War, the last perhaps of the autocrats with a mystical belief in the divine character of his mission, showed some interest in this pair of married lovers. It is true that Nicholas kept a watchful eye on all the doings of the great Polish nobles. The young people leading a life appropriate to their station were obviously wrapped up in each other; and society, fascinated by the sincerity of a feeling moving serenely among the artificialities of its anxious and fastidious agitation, watched them with benevolent indulgence and an amused tenderness.

'The marriage was the social event of 1828, in the capital. Just forty years afterwards I was staying in the country house of my mother's brother in our southern provinces.

'It was the dead of winter. The great lawn in front was as pure and smooth as an alpine snowfield, a white and feathery level sparkling under the sun as if sprinkled with diamond dust, declining gently to the lake – a long, sinuous piece of frozen water looking bluish and more solid than the earth. A cold brilliant sun glided low above an undulating horizon of great folds of snow in which the villages of Ukrainian peasants remained out of sight, like clusters of boats hidden in the hollows of a running sea. And everything was very still.

'I don't know now how I had managed to escape at eleven o'clock in the morning from the schoolroom. I was a boy of eight, the little girl, my cousin, a few months younger than myself, though hereditarily more quick-tempered, was less adventurous. So I had escaped alone; and presently I found myself in the great stone-paved hall, warmed by a monumental stove of white tiles, a much more pleasant locality than the schoolroom, which for some reason or other, perhaps hygienic, was always kept at a low temperature.

'We children were aware that there was a guest staying in the house. He had arrived the night before just as we were being driven off to bed. We broke back through the line of beaters to rush and flatten our noses against the dark window panes; but we were too late to see him alight. We had only watched in a ruddy glare the big travelling carriage on sleigh runners harnessed with six horses, a black mass against the snow, going off to the stables, preceded by a horseman carrying a blazing ball of tow and resin in an iron basket at the end of a long stick swung from his saddle bow. Two stable boys had been sent out early in the afternoon along the snow tracks to meet the expected guest at dusk and light his way with these road torches. At that time, you must remember, there was not a single mile of railways in our southern provinces. My little cousin and I had no knowledge of trains and engines, except from picture books, as of things rather vague, extremely remote, and not particularly interesting unless to grownups who travelled abroad.

'Our notion of princes, perhaps a little more precise, was mainly literary and had a glamour reflected from the light of fairy tales, in which princes always appear young, charming, heroic, and fortunate. Yet, as well as any other children, we could draw a firm line between the real and the ideal. We knew that princes were historical personages. And there was some glamour in that fact, too. But what had driven me to roam cautiously over the house like an escaped prisoner was the hope of snatching an interview with a special friend of mine, the head forester, who generally came to make his report at that time of the day. I yearned for news of a certain wolf. You know, in a country where wolves are to be found, every winter almost brings forward an individual eminent by the audacity of his misdeeds, by his more perfect wolfishness – so to speak. I wanted to hear some new thrilling tale of that wolf – perhaps the dramatic story of his death…

'But there was no one in the hall.

'Deceived in my hopes, I became suddenly very much depressed. Unable to slip back in triumph to my studies I elected to stroll spiritlessly into the billiard room where certainly I had no business. There was no one there either, and I felt very lost and desolate under its high ceiling, all alone with the massive English billiard table which seemed, in heavy, rectilinear silence, to disapprove of that small boy's intrusion.

'As I began to think of retreat I heard footsteps in the adjoining drawing room; and, before I could turn tail and flee, my uncle and his guest appeared in the doorway. To run away after having been seen would have been highly improper, so I stood my ground. My uncle looked surprised to see me; the guest by his side was a spare man, of average stature, buttoned up in a black frock coat and holding himself very erect with a stiffly soldier-like carriage. From the folds of a soft white cambric neck cloth peeped the points of a collar close against each shaven cheek. A few wisps of thin grey hair were brushed smoothly across the top of his bald head. His face, which must have been beautiful in its day, had preserved in age the harmonious simplicity of its lines. What amazed me was its even, almost deathlike pallor. He seemed to me to be prodigiously old. A faint smile, a mere momentary alteration in the set of his thin lips acknowledged my blushing confusion; and I became greatly interested to see him reach into the inside breast pocket of his coat. He extracted therefrom a lead pencil and a block of detachable pages, which he handed to my uncle with an almost imperceptible bow.

'I was very much astonished, but my uncle received it as a matter of course. He wrote something at which the other glanced and nodded slightly. A thin wrinkled hand – the hand was older than the face – patted my cheek and then rested on my head lightly. An un-ringing voice, a voice as colourless as the face itself, issued from his sunken lips, while the eyes, dark and still, looked down at me kindly.

'"And how old is this shy little boy?"

'Before I could answer my uncle wrote down my age on the pad. I was deeply impressed. What was this ceremony? Was this personage too great to be spoken to? Again he glanced at the pad, and again gave a nod, and again that impersonal, mechanical voice was heard, "He resembles his grandfather."

'I remembered my paternal grandfather. He had died not long before. He, too, was prodigiously old. And to me it seemed perfectly natural that two such ancient and venerable persons should have known each other in the dim ages of creation before my birth. But my uncle obviously had not been aware of the fact. So obviously that the mechanical voice explained, "Yes, yes. Comrades in '31. He was one of those who knew. Old times, my dear sir, old times…"

'He made a gesture as if to put aside an importunate ghost. And now they were both looking down at me. I wondered whether anything was expected from me. To my round, questioning eyes my uncle remarked, "He's completely deaf." And the unrelated, inexpressive voice said, "Give me your hand."

'Acutely conscious of inky fingers I put it out timidly. I had never seen a deaf person before and was rather startled. He pressed it firmly and then gave me a final pat on the head.

'My uncle addressed me weightily, "You have shaken hands with Prince Roman S—. It's something for you to remember when you grow up."

'I was impressed by his tone. I had enough historical information to know vaguely that the Princes S— counted amongst the sovereign Princes of Ruthenia till the union of all Ruthenian lands to the kingdom of Poland, when they became great Polish magnates, sometime at the beginning of the 15th Century. But what concerned me most was the failure of the fairy-tale glamour. It was shocking to discover a prince who was deaf, bald, meagre, and so prodigiously old. It never occurred to me that this imposing and disappointing man had been young, rich, beautiful; I could not know that he had been happy in the felicity of an ideal marriage uniting two young hearts, two great names and two great fortunes; happy with a happiness which, as in fairy tales, seemed destined to last for ever...

'But it did not last for ever. It was fated not to last very long even by the measure of the days allotted to men's passage on this earth where enduring happiness is only found in the conclusion of fairy tales. A daughter was born to them and shortly afterwards, the health of the young princess began to fail. For a time she bore up with smiling intrepidity, sustained by the feeling that now her existence was necessary for the happiness of two lives. But at last the husband, thoroughly alarmed by the rapid changes in her appearance, obtained an unlimited leave and took her away from the capital to his parents in the country.

'The old prince and princess were extremely frightened at the state of their beloved daughter-in-law. Preparations were at once made for a journey abroad. But it seemed as if it were already too late; and the invalid herself opposed the project with gentle obstinacy. Thin and pale in the great armchair, where the insidious and obscure nervous malady made her appear smaller and more frail every day without effacing the smile of her eyes or the charming grace of her wasted face, she clung to her native land and wished to breathe her native air. Nowhere else could she expect to get well so quickly, nowhere else would it be so easy for her to die.

'She died before her little girl was two years old. The grief of the husband was terrible and the more alarming to his parents because perfectly silent and dry-eyed. After the funeral, while the immense bareheaded crowd of peasants surrounding the private chapel on the grounds was dispersing, the Prince, waving away his friends and relations, remained alone to watch the masons of the estate closing the family vault. When the last stone was in position he uttered a groan, the first sound of pain which had escaped from him for days, and walking away with lowered head shut himself up again in his apartments.

'His father and mother feared for his reason. His outward tranquillity was appalling to them. They had nothing to trust to but that very youth which made his despair so self-absorbed and so intense. Old Prince John, fretful and anxious, repeated, "Poor Roman should be roused somehow. He's so young." But they could find nothing to rouse him with. And the old princess, wiping her eyes, wished in her heart he were young enough to come and cry at her knee.

'In time Prince Roman, making an effort, would join now and again the family circle. But it was as if his heart and his mind had been buried in the family vault with the wife he had lost. He took to wandering in the woods with a gun, watched over secretly by one of the keepers, who would report in the evening that "His Serenity has never fired a shot all day." Sometimes walking to the stables in the morning he would order in subdued tones a horse to be saddled, wait switching his boot till it was led up to him, then mount without a word and ride out of the gates at a walking pace. He would be gone all day. People saw him on the roads looking neither to the right nor to the left, white faced, sitting rigidly in the saddle like a horseman of stone on a living mount.

'The peasants working in the fields, the great unhedged fields, looked after him from the distance; and sometimes some sympathetic old woman on the threshold of a low, thatched hut was moved to make the sign of the cross in the air behind his back; as though he were one of themselves, a simple village soul struck by a sore affliction.

'He rode looking straight ahead seeing no one as if the earth were empty and all mankind buried in that grave which had opened so suddenly in his path to swallow up his happiness. What were men to him with their sorrows, joys, labours and passions from which she who had been all the world to him had been cut off so early?

'They did not exist; and he would have felt as completely lonely and abandoned as a man in the toils of a cruel nightmare if it had not been for this countryside where he had been born and had spent his happy boyish years. He knew it well – every slight rise crowned with trees amongst the ploughed fields, every dell concealing a village. The dammed streams made a chain of lakes set in the green meadows. Far away to the north the great Lithuanian forest faced the sun, no higher than a hedge; and to the south, the way to the plains, the vast brown spaces of the earth touched the blue sky.

'And this familiar landscape associated with the days without thought and without sorrow, this land the charm of which he felt without even looking at it soothed his pain, like the presence of an old friend who sits silent and disregarded by one in some dark hour of life.

'One afternoon, it happened that the Prince after turning his horse's head for home remarked a low dense cloud of dark dust cutting off slantwise a part of the view. He reined in on a knoll and peered. There were slender gleams of steel here and there in that cloud, and it contained moving forms which revealed themselves at last as a long line of peasant carts full of soldiers, moving slowly in double file under the escort of mounted Cossacks.

'It was like an immense reptile creeping over the fields; its head dipped out of sight in a slight hollow and its tail went on writhing and growing shorter as though the monster were eating its way slowly into the very heart of the land.

'The Prince directed his way through a village lying a little off the track. The roadside inn with its stable, byre, and barn under one enormous thatched roof resembled a deformed, hunchbacked, ragged giant, sprawling amongst the small huts of the peasants. The innkeeper, a portly, dignified Jew, clad in a black satin coat reaching down to his heels and girt with a red sash, stood at the door stroking his long silvery beard.

'He watched the Prince approach and bowed gravely from the waist, not expecting to be noticed even, since it was well known that their young lord had no eyes for anything or anybody in his grief. It was quite a shock for him when the Prince pulled up and asked:

'"What's all this, Yankel?"

'"That is, please your Serenity, that is a convoy of foot-soldiers they are hurrying down to the south."

'He glanced right and left cautiously, but as there was no one near but some children playing in the dust of the village street, he came up close to the stirrup.

'"Doesn't your Serenity know? It has begun already down there. All the landowners great and small are out in arms and even the common people have risen. Only yesterday the saddler from Grodek (it was a tiny market-town near by) went through here with his two apprentices on his way to join. He left even his cart with me. I gave him a guide through our neighbourhood. You know, your Serenity, our people they travel a lot and they see all that's going on, and they know all the roads."

'He tried to keep down his excitement, for the Jew Yankel, innkeeper and tenant of all the mills on the estate, was a Polish patriot. And in a still lower voice:

'"I was already a married man when the French and all the other nations passed this way with Napoleon. Tse! Tse! That was a great harvest for death, *nu!* Perhaps this time God will help."

'The Prince nodded. "Perhaps" – and falling into deep meditation he let his horse take him home.

'That night he wrote a letter, and early in the morning sent a mounted express to the post town. During the day he came out of his taciturnity, to the great joy of the family circle, and conversed with his father of recent events – the revolt in Warsaw, the flight of the Grand Duke Constantine, the first slight successes of the Polish army (at that time there was a Polish army); the risings in the provinces. Old Prince John, moved and uneasy, speaking from a purely aristocratic point of view, mistrusted the popular origins of the movement, regretted its democratic tendencies, and did not believe in the possibility of success. He was sad, inwardly agitated.

'"I am judging all this calmly. There are secular principles of legitimity and order which have been violated in this reckless enterprise for the sake of most subversive illusions. Though of course the patriotic impulses of the heart…"

'Prince Roman had listened in a thoughtful attitude. He took advantage of the pause to tell his father quietly that he had sent that morning a letter to St Petersburg resigning his commission in the Guards.

'The old prince remained silent. He thought that he ought to have been consulted. His son was also ordnance officer to the Emperor and he knew that the Tsar would never forget this appearance of defection in a Polish noble. In a discontented tone he pointed out to his son that as it was he had an unlimited leave. The right thing would have been to keep quiet. They had too much tact at Court to recall a man of his name. Or at worst some distant mission might have been asked for – to the Caucasus for instance – away from this unhappy struggle which was wrong in principle and therefore destined to fail.

'"Presently you shall find yourself without any interest in life and with no occupation. And you shall need something to occupy you, my poor boy. You have acted rashly, I fear."

'Prince Roman murmured.

'"I thought it better."

'His father faltered under his steady gaze.

'"Well, well – perhaps! But as ordnance officer to the Emperor and in favour with all the Imperial family…"

'"Those people had never been heard of when our house was already illustrious,' the young man let fall disdainfully.

'This was the sort of remark to which the old prince was sensible.

'"Well – perhaps it is better," he conceded at last.

'The father and son parted affectionately for the night. The next day Prince Roman seemed to have fallen back into the depths of his indifference. He rode out as usual. He remembered that the day before he had seen a reptile-like convoy of soldiery, bristling with bayonets, crawling over the face of that land which was his. The woman he loved had been his, too. Death had robbed him of her. Her loss had been to him a moral shock. It had opened his heart to a greater sorrow, his mind to a vaster thought, his eyes to all the past and to the existence of another love fraught with pain but as mysteriously imperative as that lost one to which he had entrusted his happiness.

'That evening he retired earlier than usual and rang for his personal servant.

'"Go and see if there is light yet in the quarters of the Master of the Horse. If he is still up ask him to come and speak to me."

'While the servant was absent on this errand the Prince tore up hastily some papers, locked the drawers of his desk, and hung a medallion, containing the miniature of his wife, round his neck against his breast.

'The man the Prince was expecting belonged to that past which the death of his love had called to life. He was of a family of small nobles who for generations had been adherents, servants, and friends of the Princes S—. He remembered the times before the last partition and had taken part in the struggles of the last hour. He was a typical old Pole of that class, with a great capacity for emotion, for blind enthusiasm; with martial instincts and simple beliefs; and even with the old-time habit of larding his speech with Latin words. And his kindly shrewd eyes, his ruddy face, his lofty brow and his thick, grey, pendent moustache were also very typical of his kind.

'"Listen, Master Francis," the Prince said familiarly and without preliminaries. "Listen, old friend. I am going to vanish from here quietly. I go where something louder than my grief and yet something with a voice very like it calls me. I confide in you alone. You will say what's necessary when the time comes."

'The old man understood. His extended hands trembled exceedingly. But as soon as he found his voice he thanked God aloud for letting him live long enough to see the descendant of the illustrious family in its youngest generation give an example *coram gentibus* of the love of his country and of valour in the field. He doubted not of his dear Prince attaining a place in council and in war worthy of his high birth; he saw already that *in fulgore* of family glory *affulget patride serenitas*. At the end of the speech he burst into tears and fell into the Prince's arms.

'The Prince quieted the old man and when he had him seated in an armchair and comparatively composed he said:

'"Don't misunderstand me, Master Francis. You know how I loved my wife. A loss like that opens one's eyes to unsuspected truths. There is no question here of leadership and glory. I mean to go alone and to fight obscurely in the ranks. I am going to offer my country what is mine to offer, that is my life, as simply as the saddler from Grodek who went through yesterday with his apprentices."

'The old man cried out at this. That could never be. He could not allow it. But he had to give way before the arguments and the express will of the Prince. "Ha! If you say that it is a matter of feeling and conscience – so be it. But you cannot go utterly alone. Alas! that I am too old to be of any use. *Cripit verba dolor*, my dear Prince, at the thought that I am over seventy and of no more account in the world than a cripple in the church porch. It seems that to sit at home and pray to God for the nation and for you is all I am fit for. But there is my son, my youngest son, Peter. He will make a worthy companion for you. And as it happens he's staying with me here. There has not been for ages a Prince S— hazarding his life without a companion of our name to ride by his side. You must have by you somebody who knows who you are if only to let your parents and your old servant hear what is happening to you. And when does your Princely Mightiness mean to start?"

'"In an hour," said the Prince; and the old man hurried off to warn his son.

'Prince Roman took up a candlestick and walked quietly along a dark corridor in the silent house. The head nurse said afterwards that waking up suddenly she saw the Prince looking at his child, one hand shading the light from its eyes. He stood and gazed at her for some time, and then putting the candlestick on the floor bent over the cot and kissed lightly the little girl who did not wake. He went out noiselessly, taking the light away with him. She saw his face perfectly well, but she could read nothing of his purpose in it. It was pale but perfectly calm and after he turned away from the cot he never looked back at it once.

'The only other trusted person, besides the old man and his son Peter, was the Jew Yankel. When he asked the Prince where precisely he wanted to be guided the Prince answered, "To the nearest party." A grandson of the Jew, a lanky youth, conducted the two young men by little-known paths across woods and morasses, and led them in sight of the few fires of a small detachment camped in a hollow. Some invisible horses neighed, a voice in the dark cried, "Who goes there?"... and the young Jew departed hurriedly, explaining that he must make haste home to be in time for keeping the Sabbath.

'Thus humbly and in accord with the simplicity of the vision of duty he saw when death had removed the brilliant bandage of happiness from his eyes, did Prince Roman bring his offering to his country. His companion made himself known as the son of the Master of the Horse to the Princes S— and declared him to be a relation, a distant cousin from the same parts as himself and, as people presumed, of the same name. In truth no one inquired much. Two more young men clearly of the right sort had joined. Nothing more natural.

'Prince Roman did not remain long in the south. One day while scouting with several others, they were ambushed near the entrance of a village by some Russian infantry. The first discharge laid low a good many and the rest scattered in all directions. The Russians, too, did not stay, being afraid of a return in force. After some time, the peasants coming to view the scene extricated Prince Roman from under his dead horse. He was unhurt but his faithful companion had been one of the first to fall. The Prince helped the peasants to bury him and the other dead.

'Then alone, not certain where to find the body of partisans which was constantly moving about in all directions, he resolved to try and join the main Polish army facing the Russians on the borders of Lithuania. Disguised in peasant clothes, in case of meeting some marauding Cossacks, he wandered a couple of weeks before he came upon a village occupied by a regiment of Polish cavalry on outpost duty.

'On a bench, before a peasant hut of a better sort, sat an elderly officer whom he took for the colonel. The Prince approached respectfully, told his story shortly and stated his desire to enlist; and when asked his name by the officer, who had been looking him over carefully, he gave on the spur of the moment the name of his dead companion.

'The elderly officer thought to himself: Here's the son of some peasant proprietor of the liberated class. He liked his appearance.

'"And can you read and write, my good fellow?" he asked.

'"Yes, your honour, I can," said the Prince.

'"Good. Come along inside the hut; the regimental adjutant is there. He will enter your name and administer the oath to you."

'The adjutant stared very hard at the newcomer but said nothing. When all the forms had been gone through and the recruit gone out, he turned to his superior officer.

'"Do you know who that is?"

'"Who? That Peter? A likely chap."

'"That's Prince Roman S—."

'"Nonsense."

'But the adjutant was positive. He had seen the Prince several times, about two years before, in the Castle in Warsaw. He had even spoken to him once at a reception of officers held by the Grand Duke.

'"He's changed. He seems much older, but I am certain of my man. I have a good memory for faces."

'The two officers looked at each other in silence.

'"He's sure to be recognised sooner or later," murmured the adjutant. The colonel shrugged his shoulders.

'"It's no affair of ours – if he has a fancy to serve in the ranks. As to being recognised it's not so likely. All our officers and men come from the other end of Poland."

'He meditated gravely for a while, then smiled. "He told me he could read and write. There's nothing to prevent me making him a sergeant at the first opportunity. He's sure to shape all right."

'Prince Roman as a non-commissioned officer surpassed the colonel's expectations. Before long Sergeant Peter became famous for his resourcefulness and courage. It was not the reckless courage of a desperate man; it was a self-possessed, as if conscientious, valour which nothing could dismay; a boundless but equable devotion, unaffected by time, by reverses, by the discouragement of endless retreats, by the bitterness of waning hopes and the horrors of pestilence added to the toils and perils of war. It was in this year that the cholera made its first appearance in Europe. It devastated the camps of both armies, affecting the firmest minds with the terror of a mysterious death stalking silently between the piled up arms and around the bivouac fires.

'A sudden shriek would wake up the harassed soldiers and they would see in the glow of embers one of themselves writhe on the ground like a worm trodden on by an invisible foot. And before the dawn broke he would be stiff and cold. Parties so visited have been known to rise like one man, abandon the fire and run off into the night in mute panic. Or a comrade talking to you on the march would stammer suddenly in the middle of a sentence, roll affrighted eyes, and fall down with distorted face and blue lips, breaking the ranks with the convulsions of his agony. Men were struck in the saddle, on sentry duty, in the firing line, carrying orders, serving the guns. I have been told that in a battalion forming under fire with perfect steadiness for the assault of a village, three cases occurred within five minutes at the head of the column; and the attack could not be delivered because the leading companies scattered all over the fields like chaff before the wind.

'Sergeant Peter, young as he was, had a great influence over his men. It was said that the number of desertions in the squadron in which he served was less than in any other in the whole of that cavalry division. Such was supposed to be the compelling example of one man's quiet intrepidity in facing every form of danger and terror.

'However that may be, he was liked and trusted generally. When the end came and the remnants of that army corps, hard pressed on all sides, were preparing to cross the Prussian frontier, Sergeant Peter had enough influence to rally round him a score of troopers. He managed to escape with them at night, from the hemmed-in army. He led this band through 200 miles of country covered by numerous Russian detachments and ravaged by the cholera. But this was not to avoid captivity, to go into hiding and try to save themselves. No. He led them into a fortress which was still occupied by the Poles, and where the last stand of the vanquished revolution was to be made.

'This looks like mere fanaticism. But fanaticism is human. Man has adored ferocious divinities. There is ferocity in every passion, even in love itself. The religion of undying hope resembles the mad cult of despair, of death, of annihilation. The difference lies in the moral motive springing from the secret needs and the unexpressed aspiration of the believers. It is only to vain men that all is vanity; and all is deception only to those who have never been sincere with themselves.

'It was in the fortress that my grandfather found himself together with Sergeant Peter. My grandfather was a neighbour of the S— family in the country but he did not know Prince Roman, who however knew his name perfectly well. The Prince introduced himself one night as they both sat on the ramparts, leaning against a gun carriage.

'The service he wished to ask for was, in case of his being killed, to have the intelligence conveyed to his parents.

'They talked in low tones, the other servants of the piece lying about near them. My grandfather gave the required promise, and then asked frankly – for he was greatly interested by the disclosure so unexpectedly made:

'"But tell me, Prince, why this request? Have you any evil forebodings as to yourself?"

'"Not in the least; I was thinking of my people. They have no idea where I am," answered Prince Roman. "I'll engage to do as much for you, if you like. It's certain that half of us at least shall be killed before the end, so there's an even chance of one of us surviving the other."

'My grandfather told him where, as he supposed, his wife and children were then. From that moment till the end of the siege the two were much together. On the day of the great assault my grandfather received a severe wound. The town was taken. Next day the citadel itself, its hospital full of dead and dying, its magazines empty, its defenders having burnt their last cartridge, opened its gates.

'During all the campaign the Prince, exposing his person conscientiously on every occasion, had not received a scratch. No one had recognised him or at any rate had betrayed his identity. Till then, as long as he did his duty, it had mattered nothing who he was.

'Now, however, the position was changed. As ex-guardsman and as late ordnance officer to the Emperor, this rebel ran a serious risk of being given special attention in the shape of a firing squad at ten paces. For more than a month he remained lost in the miserable crowd of prisoners packed in the casemates of the citadel, with just enough food to keep body and soul together but otherwise allowed to die from wounds, privation, and disease at the rate of forty or so a day.

'The position of the fortress being central, new parties, captured in the open in the course of a thorough pacification, were being sent in frequently. Amongst such newcomers there happened to be a young man, a personal friend of the Prince from his school days. He recognised him, and in the extremity of his dismay cried aloud, "My God! Roman, you here!"

'It is said that years of life embittered by remorse paid for this momentary lack of self-control. All this happened in the main quadrangle of the citadel. The warning gesture of the Prince came too late. An officer of the gendarmes on guard had heard the exclamation. The incident appeared to him worth inquiring into. The investigation which followed was not very arduous because the Prince, asked categorically for his real name, owned up at once.

'The intelligence of the Prince S— being found amongst the prisoners was sent to St Petersburg. His parents were already there living in sorrow, incertitude, and apprehension. The capital of the Empire was the safest place to reside in for a noble whose son had disappeared so mysteriously from home in a time of rebellion. The old people had not heard from him, or of him, for months. They took care not to contradict the rumours of suicide from despair circulating in the great world, which remembered the interesting love match, the charming and frank happiness brought to an end by death. But they hoped secretly that their son survived, and that he had been able to cross the frontier with that part of the army which had surrendered to the Prussians.

'The news of his captivity was a crushing blow. Directly, nothing could be done for him. But the greatness of their name, of their position, their wide relations and connections in the highest spheres, enabled his parents to act indirectly and they moved heaven and earth, as the saying is, to save their son from the "consequences of his madness," as poor Prince John did not hesitate to express himself. Great personages were approached by society leaders, high dignitaries were interviewed, powerful officials were induced to take an interest in that affair. The help of every possible secret influence was enlisted. Some private secretaries got heavy bribes. The mistress of a certain senator obtained a large sum of money.

'But, as I have said, in such a glaring case no direct appeal could be made and no open steps taken. All that could be done was to incline by private representation the mind of the President of the Military Commission to the side of clemency. He ended by being impressed by the hints and suggestions, some of them from very high quarters, which he received from St Petersburg. And, after all, the gratitude of such great nobles as the Princes S— was something worth having from a worldly point of view. He was a good Russian but he was also a good-natured man. Moreover, the hate of Poles was not at that time a cardinal article of patriotic creed as it became some thirty years later. He felt well disposed at first sight towards that young man, bronzed, thin-faced, worn out by months of hard campaigning, the hardships of the siege and the rigours of captivity.

'The Commission was composed of three officers. It sat in the citadel in a bare vaulted room behind a long black table. Some clerks occupied the two ends, and besides the gendarmes who brought in the Prince there was no one else there.

'Within those four sinister walls shutting out from him all the sights and sounds of liberty, all hopes of the future, all consoling illusions – alone in the face of his enemies erected for judges, who can tell how much love of life there was in Prince Roman? How much remained in that sense of duty, revealed to him in sorrow? How much of his awakened love for his native country? That country which demands to be loved as no other country has ever been loved, with the mournful affection one bears to the unforgotten dead and with the unextinguishable fire of a hopeless passion which only a living, breathing, warm ideal can kindle in our breasts for our pride, for our weariness, for our exultation, for our undoing.

'There is something monstrous in the thought of such an exaction till it stands before us embodied in the shape of a fidelity without fear and without reproach. Nearing the supreme moment of his life the Prince could only have had the feeling that it was about to end. He answered the questions put to him clearly, concisely – with the most profound indifference. After all those tense months of action, to talk was a weariness to him. But he concealed it, lest his foes should suspect in his manner the apathy of discouragement or the numbness of a crushed spirit. The details of his conduct could have no importance one way or another; with his thoughts these men had nothing to do. He preserved a scrupulously courteous tone. He had refused the permission to sit down.

'What happened at this preliminary examination is only known from the presiding officer. Pursuing the only possible course in that glaringly bad case he tried from the first to bring to the Prince's mind the line of defence he wished him to take. He absolutely framed his questions so as to put the right answers in the culprit's mouth, going so far as to suggest the very words: how, distracted by excessive grief after his young wife's death, rendered irresponsible for his conduct by his despair, in a moment of blind recklessness, without realising the highly reprehensible nature of the act, nor yet its danger and its dishonour, he went off to join the nearest rebels on a sudden impulse. And that now, penitently...

'But Prince Roman was silent. The military judges looked at him hopefully. In silence he reached for a pen and wrote on a sheet of paper he found under his hand, "I joined the national rising from conviction."

'He pushed the paper across the table. The president took it up, showed it in turn to his two colleagues sitting to the right and left, then looking fixedly at Prince Roman let it fall from his hand. And the silence remained unbroken till he spoke to the gendarmes ordering them to remove the prisoner.

'Such was the written testimony of Prince Roman in the supreme moment of his life. I have heard that the Princes of the

S— family, in all its branches, adopted the last two words, "From conviction" for the device under the armorial bearings of their house. I don't know whether the report is true. My uncle could not tell me. He remarked only, that naturally, it was not to be seen on Prince Roman's own seal.

'He was condemned for life to Siberian mines. Emperor Nicholas, who always took personal cognizance of all sentences on Polish nobility, wrote with his own hand in the margin, "The authorities are severely warned to take care that this convict walks in chains like any other criminal every step of the way."

'It was a sentence of deferred death. Very few survived entombment in these mines for more than three years. Yet as he was reported as still alive at the end of that time he was allowed, on a petition of his parents and by way of exceptional grace, to serve as common soldier in the Caucasus. All communication with him was forbidden. He had no civil rights. For all practical purposes except that of suffering he was a dead man. The little child he had been so careful not to wake up when he kissed her in her cot, inherited all the fortune after Prince John's death. Her existence saved those immense estates from confiscation.

'It was twenty-five years before Prince Roman, stone deaf, his health broken, was permitted to return to Poland. His daughter married splendidly to a Polish Austrian *grand seigneur* and, moving in the cosmopolitan sphere of the highest European aristocracy, lived mostly abroad in Nice and Vienna. He, settling down on one of her estates, not the one with the palatial residence but another where there was a modest little house, saw very little of her.

'But Prince Roman did not shut himself up as if his work were done. There was hardly anything done in the private and public life of the neighbourhood, in which Prince Roman's advice and assistance were not called upon, and never in vain. It was well said that his days did not belong to himself but to his fellow citizens. And especially he was the particular friend of all returned exiles, helping them with purse and advice, arranging their affairs and finding them means of livelihood.

'I heard from my uncle many tales of his devoted activity, in which he was always guided by a simple wisdom, a high sense of honour, and the most scrupulous conception of private and public probity. He remains a living figure for me because of that meeting in a billiard room, when, in my anxiety to hear about a particularly wolfish wolf, I came in momentary contact with a man who was preeminently a man amongst all men capable of feeling deeply, of believing steadily, of loving ardently.

'I remember to this day the grasp of Prince Roman's bony, wrinkled hand closing on my small inky paw, and my uncle's half-serious, half-amused way of looking down at his trespassing nephew.

'They moved on and forgot that little boy. But I did not move; I gazed after them, not so much disappointed as disconcerted by this prince so utterly unlike a prince in a fairy tale. They moved very slowly across the room. Before reaching the other door the Prince stopped, and I heard him – I seem to hear him now – saying, "I wish you would write to Vienna about filling up that post. He's a most deserving fellow – and your recommendation would be decisive."

'My uncle's face turned to him expressed genuine wonder. It said as plainly as any speech could say: What better recommendation than a father's can be needed? The Prince was quick at reading expressions. Again he spoke with the toneless accent of a man who has not heard his own voice for years, for whom the soundless world is like an abode of silent shades.

'And to this day I remember the very words: "I ask you because, you see, my daughter and my son-in-law don't believe me to be a good judge of men. They think that I let myself be guided too much by mere sentiment."'

The Tale

Outside the large single window the crepuscular light was dying out slowly in a great square gleam without colour, framed rigidly in the gathering shades of the room.

It was a long room. The irresistible tide of the night ran into the most distant part of it, where the whispering of a man's voice, passionately interrupted and passionately renewed, seemed to plead against the answering murmurs of infinite sadness.

At last no answering murmur came. His movement when he rose slowly from his knees by the side of the deep, shadowy couch holding the shadowy suggestion of a reclining woman revealed him tall under the low ceiling, and sombre all over except for the crude discord of the white collar under the shape of his head and the faint, minute spark of a brass button here and there on his uniform.

He stood over her a moment, masculine and mysterious in his immobility, before he sat down on a chair near by. He could see only the faint oval of her upturned face and, extended on her black dress, her pale hands, a moment before abandoned to his kisses and now as if too weary to move.

He dared not make a sound, shrinking as a man would do from the prosaic necessities of existence. As usual, it was the woman who had the courage. Her voice was heard first – almost conventional while her being vibrated yet with conflicting emotions.

'Tell me something,' she said.

The darkness hid his surprise and then his smile. Had he not just said to her everything worth saying in the world – and that not for the first time!

'What am I to tell you?' he asked, in a voice creditably steady. He was beginning to feel grateful to her for that something final in her tone which had eased the strain.

'Why not tell me a tale?'

'A tale!' He was really amazed.

'Yes. Why not?'

These words came with a slight petulance, the hint of a loved woman's capricious will, which is capricious only because it feels itself to be a law, embarrassing sometimes and always difficult to elude.

'Why not?' he repeated, with a slightly mocking accent, as though he had been asked to give her the moon. But now he was feeling a little angry with her for that feminine mobility that slips out of an emotion as easily as out of a splendid gown.

He heard her say, a little unsteadily with a sort of fluttering intonation which made him think suddenly of a butterfly's flight:

'You used to tell – your – your simple and – and professional – tales very well at one time. Or well enough to interest me. You had a – a sort of art – in the days – the days before the war.'

'Really?' he said, with involuntary gloom. 'But now, you see, the war is going on,' he continued in such a dead, equable tone that she felt a slight chill fall over her shoulders. And yet she persisted. For there's nothing more unswerving in the world than a woman's caprice.

'It could be a tale not of this world,' she explained.

'You want a tale of the other, the better world?' he asked, with a matter-of-fact surprise. 'You must evoke for that task those who have already gone there.'

'No. I don't mean that. I mean another – some other – world. In the universe – not in heaven.'

'I am relieved. But you forget that I have only five days' leave.'

'Yes. And I've also taken a five days' leave from – from my duties.'

'I like that word.'

'What word?'

'Duty.'

'It is horrible – sometimes.'

'Oh, that's because you think it's narrow. But it isn't. It contains infinities, and – and so –'

'What is this jargon?'

He disregarded the interjected scorn. 'An infinity of absolution, for instance,' he continued. 'But as to this "another world" – who's going to look for it and for the tale that is in it?'

'You,' she said, with a strange, almost rough, sweetness of assertion.

He made a shadowy movement of assent in his chair, the irony of which not even the gathered darkness could render mysterious.

'As you will. In that world, then, there was once upon a time a Commanding Officer and a Northman. Put in the capitals, please, because they had no other names. It was a world of seas and continents and islands –'

'Like the earth,' she murmured, bitterly.

'Yes. What else could you expect from sending a man made of our common, tormented clay on a voyage of discovery? What else could he find? What else could you understand or care for, or feel the existence of even? There was comedy in it, and slaughter.'

'Always like the earth,' she murmured. 'Always. And since I could find in the universe only what was deeply rooted in the fibres of my being there was love in it, too. But we won't talk of that.'

'No. We won't,' she said, in a neutral tone which concealed perfectly her relief – or her disappointment. Then after a pause she added, 'It's going to be a comic story.'

'Well –' he paused, too. 'Yes. In a way. In a very grim way. It will be human, and, as you know, comedy is but a matter of the visual angle. And it won't be a noisy story. All the long guns in it will be dumb – as dumb as so many telescopes.'

'Ah, there are guns in it, then! And may I ask – where?'

'Afloat. You remember that the world of which we speak had its seas. A war was going on in it. It was a funny world and terribly in earnest. Its war was being carried on over the land, over the water, under the water, up in the air, and even under the ground. And many young men in it, mostly in wardrooms and mess rooms, used to say to each other – pardon the unparliamentary word – they used to say, "It's a damned bad war, but it's better than no war at all." Sounds flippant, doesn't it?'

He heard a nervous, impatient sigh in the depths of the couch while he went on without a pause.

'And yet there is more in it than meets the eye. I mean more wisdom. Flippancy, like comedy, is but a matter of visual first impression. That world was not very wise. But there was in it a certain amount of common working sagacity. That, however, was mostly worked by the neutrals in diverse ways, public and private, which had to be watched; watched by acute minds and also by actual sharp eyes. They had to be very sharp indeed, too, I assure you.'

'I can imagine,' she murmured, appreciatively.

'What is there that you can't imagine?' he pronounced, soberly. 'You have the world in you. But let us go back to our commanding officer, who, of course, commanded a ship of a sort. My tales if often professional (as you remarked just now) have never been technical. So I'll just tell you that the ship was of a very ornamental sort once, with lots of grace and elegance and luxury about her. Yes, once! She was like a pretty woman who had suddenly put on a suit of sackcloth and stuck revolvers in her belt. But she floated lightly, she moved nimbly, she was quite good enough.'

'That was the opinion of the commanding officer?' said the voice from the couch.

'It was. He used to be sent out with her along certain coasts to see – what he could see. Just that. And sometimes he had some preliminary information to help him, and sometimes he had not. And it was all one, really. It was about as useful as information trying to convey the locality and intentions of a cloud, of a phantom taking shape here and there and impossible to seize, would have been.

'It was in the early days of the war. What at first used to amaze the commanding officer was the unchanged face of the waters, with its familiar expression, neither more friendly nor more hostile. On fine days the sun strikes sparks upon the blue; here and there a peaceful smudge of smoke hangs in the distance, and it is impossible to believe that the familiar clear horizon traces the limit of one great circular ambush.

'Yes, it is impossible to believe, till some day you see a ship not your own ship (that isn't so impressive), but some ship in company, blow up all of a sudden and plop under almost before you know what has happened to her. Then you begin to believe. Henceforth you go out for the work to see – what you can see, and you keep on at it with the conviction that some day you will die from something you have not seen. One envies the soldiers at the end of the day, wiping the sweat and blood from their faces, counting the dead fallen to their hands, looking at the devastated fields, the torn earth that seems to suffer and bleed with them. One does, really. The final brutality of it – the taste of primitive passion – the ferocious frankness of the blow struck with one's hand – the direct call and the straight response. Well, the sea gave you nothing of that, and seemed to pretend that there was nothing the matter with the world.'

She interrupted, stirring a little.

'Oh, yes. Sincerity – frankness – passion – three words of your gospel. Don't I know them!'

'Think! Isn't it ours – believed in common?' he asked, anxiously, yet without expecting an answer, and went on at once, 'Such were the feelings of the commanding officer. When the night came trailing over the sea, hiding what looked like the hypocrisy of an old friend, it was a relief. The night blinds you frankly – and there are circumstances when the sunlight may grow as odious to one as falsehood itself. Night is all right.

'At night the commanding officer could let his thoughts get away – I won't tell you where. Somewhere where there was no choice but between truth and death. But thick weather, though it blinded one, brought no such relief. Mist is deceitful, the dead luminosity of the fog is irritating. It seems that you *ought* to see.

'One gloomy, nasty day the ship was steaming along her beat in sight of a rocky, dangerous coast that stood out intensely black like an India ink drawing on grey paper. Presently the second in command spoke to his chief. He thought he saw something on the water, to seaward. Small wreckage, perhaps.

'"But there shouldn't be any wreckage here, sir," he remarked.

'"No," said the commanding officer. "The last reported submarined ships were sunk a long way to the westward. But one never knows. There may have been others since then not reported nor seen. Gone with all hands."

'That was how it began. The ship's course was altered to pass the object close; for it was necessary to have a good look at what one could see. Close, but without touching; for it was not advisable to come in contact with objects of any form whatever floating casually about. Close, but without stopping or even diminishing speed; for in those times it was not prudent to linger on any particular spot, even for a moment. I may tell you at once that the object was not dangerous in itself. No use in describing it. It may have been nothing more remarkable than, say, a barrel of a certain shape and colour. But it was significant.

'The smooth bow wave hove it up as if for a closer inspection, and then the ship, brought again to her course, turned her back on it with indifference, while twenty pairs of eyes on her deck stared in all directions trying to see – what they could see.

'The commanding officer and his second in command discussed the object with understanding. It appeared to them to be not so much a proof of the sagacity as of the activity of certain neutrals. This activity had in many cases taken the form of replenishing the stores of certain submarines at sea. This was generally believed, if not absolutely known. But the very nature of things in those early days pointed that way. The object, looked at closely and turned away from with apparent indifference, put it beyond doubt that something of the sort had been done somewhere in the neighbourhood.

'The object in itself was more than suspect. But the fact of its being left in evidence roused other suspicions. Was it the result of some deep and devilish purpose? As to that all speculation soon appeared to be a vain thing. Finally the two officers came to the conclusion that it was left there most likely by accident, complicated possibly by some unforeseen necessity; such, perhaps, as the sudden need to get away quickly from the spot, or something of that kind.

'Their discussion had been carried on in curt, weighty phrases, separated by long, thoughtful silences. And all the time their eyes roamed about the horizon in an everlasting, almost mechanical effort of vigilance. The younger man summed up grimly:

'"Well, it's evidence. That's what this is. Evidence of what we were pretty certain of before. And plain, too."

'"And much good it will do to us," retorted the commanding officer. "The parties are miles away; the submarine, devil only knows where, ready to kill; and the noble neutral slipping away to the eastward, ready to lie!"

'The second in command laughed a little at the tone. But he guessed that the neutral wouldn't even have to lie very much. Fellows like that, unless caught in the very act, felt themselves pretty safe. They could afford to chuckle. That fellow was probably chuckling to himself. It's very possible he had been before at the game and didn't care a rap for the bit of evidence left behind. It was a game in which practice made one bold and successful, too.

'And again he laughed faintly. But his commanding officer was in revolt against the murderous stealthiness of methods and the atrocious callousness of complicities that seemed to taint the very source of men's deep emotions and noblest activities; to corrupt their imagination which builds up the final conceptions of life and death. He suffered –'

The voice from the sofa interrupted the narrator.

'How well I can understand that in him!'

He bent forward slightly.

'Yes. I, too. Everything should be open in love and war. Open as the day, since both are the call of an ideal which it is so easy, so terribly easy, to degrade in the name of Victory.'

He paused; then went on:

'I don't know that the commanding officer delved so deep as that into his feelings. But he did suffer from them – a sort of disenchanted sadness. It is possible, even, that he suspected himself of folly. Man is various. But he had no time for much introspection, because from the southwest a wall of fog had advanced upon his ship. Great convolutions of vapours flew over, swirling about masts and funnel, which looked as if they were beginning to melt. Then they vanished.

'The ship was stopped, all sounds ceased, and the very fog became motionless, growing denser and as if solid in its amazing dumb immobility. The men at their stations lost sight of each other. Footsteps sounded stealthy; rare voices, impersonal and remote, died out without resonance. A blind white stillness took possession of the world.

'It looked, too, as if it would last for days. I don't mean to say that the fog did not vary a little in its density. Now and then it would thin out mysteriously, revealing to the men a more or less ghostly presentment of their ship. Several times the shadow of the coast itself swam darkly before their eyes through the fluctuating opaque brightness of the great white cloud clinging to the water.

'Taking advantage of these moments, the ship had been moved cautiously nearer the shore. It was useless to remain out in such thick weather. Her officers knew every nook and cranny of the coast along their beat. They thought that she would be much better in a certain cove. It wasn't a large place, just ample room for a ship to swing at her anchor. She would have an easier time of it till the fog lifted up.

'Slowly, with infinite caution and patience, they crept closer and closer, seeing no more of the cliffs than an evanescent dark loom with a narrow border of angry foam at its foot. At the moment of anchoring the fog was so thick that for all they could see they might have been a thousand miles out in the open sea. Yet the shelter of the land could be felt. There was a peculiar quality in the stillness of the air. Very faint, very elusive, the wash of the ripple against the encircling land reached their ears, with mysterious sudden pauses.

'The anchor dropped, the leads were laid in. The commanding officer went below into his cabin. But he had not been there very long when a voice outside his door requested his presence on deck. He thought to himself, "What is it now?" He felt some impatience at being called out again to face the wearisome fog.

'He found that it had thinned again a little and had taken on a gloomy hue from the dark cliffs which had no form, no outline, but asserted themselves as a curtain of shadows all round the ship, except in one bright spot, which was the entrance from the open sea. Several officers were looking that way from the bridge. The second in command met him with the breathlessly whispered information that there was another ship in the cove.

'She had been made out by several pairs of eyes only a couple of minutes before. She was lying at anchor very near the entrance – a mere vague blot on the fog's brightness. And the commanding officer by staring in the direction pointed out to him by eager hands ended by distinguishing it at last himself. Indubitably a vessel of some sort.

'"It's a wonder we didn't run slap into her when coming in," observed the second in command.

'"Send a boat on board before she vanishes," said the commanding officer. He surmised that this was a coaster. It could hardly be anything else. But another thought came into his head suddenly. "It is a wonder," he said to his second in command, who had rejoined him after sending the boat away.

'By that time both of them had been struck by the fact that the ship so suddenly discovered had not manifested her presence by ringing her bell.

'"We came in very quietly, that's true," concluded the younger officer. "But they must have heard our leadsmen at least. We couldn't have passed her more than fifty yards off. The closest shave! They may even have made us out, since they were aware of something coming in. And the strange thing is that we never heard a sound from her. The fellows on board must have been holding their breath."

'"Aye," said the commanding officer, thoughtfully.

'In due course the boarding boat returned, appearing suddenly alongside, as though she had burrowed her way under the fog. The officer in charge came up to make his report, but the commanding officer didn't give him time to begin. He cried from a distance:

'"Coaster, isn't she?"

'"No, sir. A stranger – a neutral," was the answer.

'"No. Really! Well, tell us all about it. What is she doing here?"

'The young man stated then that he had been told a long and complicated story of engine troubles. But it was plausible enough from a strictly professional point of view and it had the usual features: disablement, dangerous drifting along the shore, weather more or less thick for days, fear of a gale, ultimately a resolve to go in and anchor anywhere on the coast, and so on. Fairly plausible.

'"Engines still disabled?" inquired the commanding officer.

'"No, sir. She has steam on them."

'The commanding officer took his second aside. "By Jove!" he said, "you were right! They were holding their breaths as we passed them. They were."

'But the second in command had his doubts now.

'"A fog like this does muffle small sounds, sir," he remarked. "And what could his object be, after all?"

'"To sneak out unnoticed," answered the commanding officer.

'"Then why didn't he? He might have done it, you know. Not exactly unnoticed, perhaps. I don't suppose he could have slipped his cable without making some noise. Still, in a minute or so he would have been lost to view – clean gone before we had made him out fairly. Yet he didn't."

'They looked at each other. The commanding officer shook his head. Such suspicions as the one which had entered his head are not defended easily. He did not even state it openly. The boarding officer finished his report. The cargo of the ship was of a harmless and useful character. She was bound to an English port. Papers and everything in perfect order. Nothing suspicious to be detected anywhere.

'Then passing to the men, he reported the crew on deck as the usual lot. Engineers of the well-known type, and very full of their achievement in repairing the engines. The mate surly. The master rather a fine specimen of a Northman, civil enough, but appeared to have been drinking. Seemed to be recovering from a regular bout of it.

'"I told him I couldn't give him permission to proceed. He said he wouldn't dare to move his ship her own length out in such weather as this, permission or no permission. I left a man on board, though."

'"Quite right."

'The commanding officer, after communing with his suspicions for a time, called his second aside.

'"What if she were the very ship which had been feeding some infernal submarine or other?" he said in an undertone.

'The other started. Then, with conviction:

'"She would get off scot-free. You couldn't prove it, sir."

'"I want to look into it myself."

'"From the report we've heard I am afraid you couldn't even make a case for reasonable suspicion, sir."

'"I'll go on board all the same."

'He had made up his mind. Curiosity is the great motive power of hatred and love. What did he expect to find? He could not have told anybody – not even himself.

'What he really expected to find there was the atmosphere, the atmosphere of gratuitous treachery, which in his view nothing could excuse; for he thought that even a passion of unrighteousness for its own sake could not excuse that. But could he detect it? Sniff it? Taste it? Receive some mysterious communication which would turn his invincible suspicions into a certitude strong enough to provoke action with all its risks?

'The master met him on the afterdeck, looming up in the fog amongst the blurred shapes of the usual ship's fittings. He was a robust Northman, bearded, and in the force of his age. A round leather cap fitted his head closely. His hands were rammed deep into the pockets of his short leather jacket. He kept them there while he explained that at sea he lived in the chart room, and led the way there, striding carelessly. Just before reaching the door under the bridge he staggered a little, recovered himself, flung it open, and stood aside, leaning his shoulder as if involuntarily against the side of the house, and staring vaguely into the fog-filled space. But he followed the commanding officer at once, flung the door to, snapped on the electric light, and hastened to thrust his hands back into his pockets, as though afraid of being seized by them either in friendship or in hostility.

'The place was stuffy and hot. The usual chart rack overhead was full, and the chart on the table was kept unrolled by an empty cup standing on a saucer half-full of some spilt dark liquid. A slightly nibbled biscuit reposed on the chronometer case. There were two settees, and one of them had been made up into a bed with a pillow and some blankets, which were now very much tumbled. The Northman let himself fall on it, his hands still in his pockets.

'"Well, here I am," he said, with a curious air of being surprised at the sound of his own voice.

'The commanding officer from the other settee observed the handsome, flushed face. Drops of fog hung on the yellow beard and moustaches of the Northman. The much darker eyebrows ran together in a puzzled frown, and suddenly he jumped up.

'"What I mean is that I don't know where I am. I really don't," he burst out, with extreme earnestness. "Hang it all! I got turned around somehow. The fog has been after me for a week. More than a week. And then my engines broke down. I will tell you how it was."

'He burst out into loquacity. It was not hurried, but it was insistent. It was not continuous for all that. It was broken by the most queer, thoughtful pauses. Each of these pauses lasted no more than a couple of seconds, and each had the profundity of an endless meditation. When he began again nothing betrayed in him the slightest consciousness of these intervals. There was the same fixed glance, the same unchanged earnestness of tone. He didn't know. Indeed, more than one of these pauses occurred in the middle of a sentence.

'The commanding officer listened to the tale. It struck him as more plausible than simple truth is in the habit of being. But that, perhaps, was prejudice. All the time the Northman was speaking the commanding officer had been aware of an inward voice, a grave murmur in the depth of his very own self, telling another tale, as if on purpose to keep alive in him his indignation and his anger with that baseness of greed or of mere outlook which lies often at the root of simple ideas.

'It was the story that had been already told to the boarding officer an hour or so before. The commanding officer nodded slightly at the Northman from time to time. The latter came to an end and turned his eyes away. He added, as an afterthought:

'"Wasn't it enough to drive a man out of his mind with worry? And it's my first voyage to this part, too. And the ship's my own. Your officer has seen the papers. She isn't much, as you can see for yourself. Just an old cargo boat. Bare living for my family."

'He raised a big arm to point at a row of photographs plastering the bulkhead. The movement was ponderous, as if the arm had been made of lead. The commanding officer said, carelessly:

'"You will be making a fortune yet for your family with this old ship."

'"Yes, if I don't lose her," said the Northman, gloomily.

'"I mean – out of this war," added the commanding officer.

'The Northman stared at him in a curiously unseeing and at the same time interested manner, as only eyes of a particular blue shade can stare.

'"And you wouldn't be angry at it," he said, "would you? You are too much of a gentleman. We didn't bring this on you. And suppose we sat down and cried. What good would that be? Let those cry who made the trouble," he concluded, with energy. "Time's money, you say. Well – *this* time *is* money. Oh! Isn't it!"

'The commanding officer tried to keep under the feeling of immense disgust. He said to himself that it was unreasonable. Men were like that – moral cannibals feeding on each other's misfortunes. He said aloud:

'"You have made it perfectly plain how it is that you are here. Your log book confirms you very minutely. Of course, a log book may be cooked. Nothing easier."

'The Northman never moved a muscle. He was gazing at the floor; he seemed not to have heard. He raised his head after a while.

'"But you can't suspect me of anything," he muttered, negligently.

'The commanding officer thought, "Why should he say this?"

'Immediately afterwards the man before him added, "My cargo is for an English port."

'His voice had turned husky for the moment. The commanding officer reflected, "That's true. There can be nothing. I can't suspect him. Yet why was he lying with steam up in this fog – and then, hearing us come in, why didn't he give some sign of life? Why? Could it be anything else but a guilty conscience? He could tell by the leadsmen that this was a man-of-war."

'Yes – why? The commanding officer went on thinking, "Suppose I ask him and then watch his face. He will betray himself in some way. It's perfectly plain that the fellow *has* been drinking. Yes, he has been drinking; but he will have a lie ready all the same." The commanding officer was one of those men who are made morally and almost physically uncomfortable by the mere thought of having to beat down a lie. He shrank from the act in scorn and disgust, which were invincible because more temperamental than moral.

'So he went out on deck instead and had the crew mustered formally for his inspection. He found them very much what the report of the boarding officer had led him to expect. And from their answers to his questions he could discover no flaw in the log book story.

'He dismissed them. His impression of them was – a picked lot; have been promised a fistful of money each if this came off; all slightly anxious, but not frightened. Not a single one of them likely to give the show away. They don't feel in danger of their life. They know England and English ways too well!

'He felt alarmed at catching himself thinking as if his vaguest suspicions were turning into a certitude. For, indeed, there was no shadow of reason for his inferences. There was nothing to give away.

'He returned to the chart room. The Northman had lingered behind there; and something subtly different in his bearing, more bold in his blue, glassy stare, induced the commanding officer to conclude that the fellow had snatched at the opportunity to take another swig at the bottle he must have had concealed somewhere.

'He noticed, too, that the Northman on meeting his eyes put on an elaborately surprised expression. At least, it seemed elaborated. Nothing could be trusted. And the Englishman felt himself with astonishing conviction faced by an enormous lie, solid like a wall, with no way round to get at the truth, whose ugly murderous face he seemed to see peeping over at him with a cynical grin.

'"I dare say," he began, suddenly, "you are wondering at my proceedings, though I am not detaining you, am I? You wouldn't dare to move in this fog?"

'"I don't know where I am," the Northman ejaculated, earnestly. "I really don't."

'He looked around as if the very chart room fittings were strange to him. The commanding officer asked him whether he had not seen any unusual objects floating about while he was at sea.

'"Objects! What objects? We were groping blind in the fog for days."

'"We had a few clear intervals," said the commanding officer. "And I'll tell you what we have seen and the conclusion I've come to about it."

'He told him in a few words. He heard the sound of a sharp breath indrawn through closed teeth. The Northman with his hand on the table stood absolutely motionless and dumb. He stood as if thunderstruck. Then he produced a fatuous smile.

'Or at least so it appeared to the commanding officer. Was this significant, or of no meaning whatever? He didn't know, he couldn't tell. All the truth had departed out of the world as if drawn in, absorbed in this monstrous villainy this man was – or was not – guilty of.

'"Shooting's too good for people that conceive neutrality in this pretty way," remarked the commanding officer, after a silence.

'"Yes, yes, yes," the Northman assented, hurriedly – then added an unexpected and dreamy-voiced "Perhaps."

'Was he pretending to be drunk, or only trying to appear sober? His glance was straight, but it was somewhat glazed. His lips outlined themselves firmly under his yellow moustache. But they twitched. Did they twitch? And why was he drooping like this in his attitude?

'"There's no perhaps about it," pronounced the commanding officer sternly.

'The Northman had straightened himself. And unexpectedly he looked stern, too.

'"No. But what about the tempters? Better kill that lot off. There's about four, five, six million of them," he said, grimly; but in a moment changed into a whining key. "But I had better hold my tongue. You have some suspicions."

'"No, I've no suspicions," declared the commanding officer.

'He never faltered. At that moment he had the certitude. The air of the chart room was thick with guilt and falsehood braving the discovery, defying simple right, common decency, all humanity of feeling, every scruple of conduct.

'The Northman drew a long breath. "Well, we know that you English are gentlemen. But let us speak the truth. Why should we love you so very much? You haven't done anything to be loved. We don't love the other people, of course. They haven't done anything for that either. A fellow comes along with a bag of gold... I haven't been in Rotterdam my last voyage for nothing."

'"You may be able to tell something interesting, then, to our people when you come into port," interjected the officer.

'"I might. But you keep some people in your pay at Rotterdam. Let them report. I am a neutral – am I not?... Have you ever seen a poor man on one side and a bag of gold on the other? Of course, I couldn't be tempted. I haven't the nerve for it. Really I haven't. It's nothing to me. I am just talking openly for once."

'"Yes. And I am listening to you," said the commanding officer, quietly.

'The Northman leaned forward over the table. "Now that I know you have no suspicions, I talk. You don't know what a poor man is. I do. I am poor myself. This old ship, she isn't much, and she is mortgaged, too. Bare living, no more. Of course, I wouldn't have the nerve. But a man who has nerve! See. The stuff he takes aboard looks like any other cargo – packages, barrels, tins, copper tubes – what not. He doesn't see it work. It isn't real to him. But he sees the gold. That's real. Of course, nothing could induce me. I suffer from an internal disease. I would either go crazy from anxiety – or – or – take to drink or something. The risk is too great. Why – ruin!"

'"It should be death." The commanding officer got up, after this curt declaration, which the other received with a hard stare oddly combined with an uncertain smile. The officer's gorge rose at the atmosphere of murderous complicity which surrounded him, denser, more impenetrable, more acrid than the fog outside.

'"It's nothing to me," murmured the Northman, swaying visibly.

'"Of course not," assented the commanding officer, with a great effort to keep his voice calm and low. The certitude was strong within him. "But I am going to clear all you fellows off this coast at once. And I will begin with you. You must leave in half an hour."

'By that time the officer was walking along the deck with the Northman at his elbow.

'"What! In this fog?" the latter cried out, huskily.

'"Yes, you will have to go in this fog."

'"But I don't know where I am. I really don't."

'The commanding officer turned round. A sort of fury possessed him. The eyes of the two men met. Those of the Northman expressed a profound amazement.

'"Oh, you don't know how to get out." The commanding officer spoke with composure, but his heart was beating with anger and dread. "I will give you your course. Steer south-by-east-half-east for about four miles and then you will be clear to haul to the eastward for your port. The weather will clear up before very long."

'"Must I? What could induce me? I haven't the nerve."

'"And yet you must go. Unless you want to – "

'"I don't want to," panted the Northman. "I've enough of it."

'The commanding officer got over the side. The Northman remained still as if rooted to the deck. Before his boat reached his ship the commanding officer heard the steamer beginning to pick up her anchor. Then, shadowy in the fog, she steamed out on the given course.

'"Yes," he said to his officers, "I let him go." '

The narrator bent forward towards the couch, where no movement betrayed the presence of a living person.

'Listen,' he said, forcibly. 'That course would lead the Northman straight on a deadly ledge of rock. And the commanding officer gave it to him. He steamed out – ran on it – and went down. So he had spoken the truth. He did not know where he was. But it proves nothing. Nothing either way. It may have been the only truth in all his story. And yet… He seems to have been driven out by a menacing stare – nothing more.'

He abandoned all pretence.

'Yes, I gave that course to him. It seemed to me a supreme test. I believe – no, I don't believe. I don't know. At the time I was certain. They all went down; and I don't know whether I have done stern retribution – or murder; whether I have added to the corpses that litter the bed of the unreadable sea the bodies of men completely innocent or basely guilty. I don't know. I shall never know.'

He rose. The woman on the couch got up and threw her arms round his neck. Her eyes put two gleams in the deep shadow of the room. She knew his passion for truth, his horror of deceit, his humanity.

'Oh, my poor, poor – '

'I shall never know,' he repeated, sternly, disengaged himself, pressed her hands to his lips, and went out.

The Black Mate

A good many years ago there were several ships loading at the Jetty, London Dock. I am speaking here of the 'eighties of the last century, of the time when London had plenty of fine ships in the docks, though not so many fine buildings in its streets.

The ships at the Jetty were fine enough; they lay one behind the other; and the *Sapphire*, third from the end, was as good as the rest of them, and nothing more. Each ship at the Jetty had, of course, her chief officer on board. So had every other ship in dock.

The policeman at the gates knew them all by sight, without being able to say at once, without thinking, to what ship any particular man belonged. As a matter of fact, the mates of the ships then lying in the London Dock were like the majority of officers in the Merchant Service – a steady, hard-working, staunch, unromantic-looking set of men, belonging to various classes of society, but with the professional stamp obliterating the personal characteristics, which were not very marked anyhow.

This last was true of them all, with the exception of the mate of the *Sapphire*. Of him the policemen could not be in doubt. This one had a presence.

He was noticeable to them in the street from a great distance; and when in the morning he strode down the Jetty to his ship, the lumpers and the dock labourers rolling the bales and trundling the cases of cargo on their hand-trucks would remark to each other:

'Here's the black mate coming along.'

That was the name they gave him, being a gross lot, who could have no appreciation of the man's dignified bearing. And to call him black was the superficial impressionism of the ignorant.

73

Of course, Mr Bunter, the mate of the *Sapphire*, was not black. He was no more black than you or I, and certainly as white as any chief mate of a ship in the whole of the Port of London. His complexion was of the sort that did not take the tan easily; and I happen to know that the poor fellow had had a month's illness just before he joined the *Sapphire*.

From this you will perceive that I knew Bunter. Of course I knew him. And, what's more, I knew his secret at the time, this secret which – never mind just now. Returning to Bunter's personal appearance, it was nothing but ignorant prejudice on the part of the foreman stevedore to say, as he did in my hearing, 'I bet he's a furriner of some sort.' A man may have black hair without being set down for a Dago. I have known a West Country sailor, boatswain of a fine ship, who looked more Spanish than any Spaniard afloat I've ever met. He looked like a Spaniard in a picture.

Competent authorities tell us that this earth is to be finally the inheritance of men with dark hair and brown eyes. It seems that already the great majority of mankind is dark-haired in various shades. But it is only when you meet one that you notice how men with really black hair, black as ebony, are rare. Bunter's hair was absolutely black, black as a raven's wing. He wore, too, all his beard (clipped, but a good length all the same), and his eyebrows were thick and bushy. Add to this steely blue eyes, which in a fair-haired man would have been nothing so extraordinary, but in that sombre framing made a startling contrast, and you will easily understand that Bunter was noticeable enough.

If it had not been for the quietness of his movements, for the general soberness of his demeanour, one would have given him credit for a fiercely passionate nature.

Of course, he was not in his first youth; but if the expression 'in the force of his age' has any meaning, he realised it completely. He was a tall man, too, though rather spare. Seeing him from his poop indefatigably busy with his duties, Captain Ashton, of the clipper ship *Elsinore*, lying just ahead of the *Sapphire*, remarked once to a friend that, 'Johns has got somebody there to hustle his ship along for him.'

Captain Johns, master of the *Sapphire*, having commanded ships for many years, was well known without being much respected or liked. In the company of his fellows he was either neglected or chaffed. The chaffing was generally undertaken by Captain Ashton, a cynical and teasing sort of man. It was Captain Ashton who permitted himself the unpleasant joke of proclaiming once in company that 'Johns is of the opinion that every sailor above forty years of age ought to be poisoned – shipmasters in actual command excepted.'

It was in a City restaurant, where several well-known shipmasters were having lunch together. There was Captain Ashton, florid and jovial, in a large white waistcoat and with a yellow rose in his buttonhole; Captain Sellers in a sack coat, thin and pale-faced, with his iron grey hair tucked behind his ears, and, but for the absence of spectacles, looking like an ascetical mild man of books; Captain Hell, a bluff sea dog with hairy fingers, in blue serge and a black felt hat pushed far back off his crimson forehead. There was also a very young shipmaster, with a little fair moustache and serious eyes, who said nothing, and only smiled faintly from time to time.

Captain Johns, very much startled, raised his perplexed and credulous glance, which, together with a low and horizontally wrinkled brow, did not make a very intellectual *ensemble*. This impression was by no means mended by the slightly pointed form of his bald head.

Everybody laughed outright, and, thus guided, Captain Johns ended by smiling rather sourly, and attempted to defend himself. It was all very well to joke, but nowadays, when ships, to pay anything at all, had to be driven hard on the passage and in harbour, the sea was no place for elderly men. Only young men and men in their prime were equal to modern conditions of push and hurry. Look at the great firms: almost every single one of them was getting rid of men showing any signs of age. He, for one, didn't want any oldsters on board his ship.

And, indeed, in this opinion Captain Johns was not singular. There was at that time a lot of seamen, with nothing against them but that they were grizzled, wearing out the soles of their last pair of boots on the pavements of the City in the heart-breaking search for a berth.

Captain Johns added with a sort of ill-humoured innocence that from holding that opinion to thinking of poisoning people was a very long step.

This seemed final but Captain Ashton would not let go his joke.

'Oh, yes. I am sure you would. You said distinctly "of no use." What's to be done with men who are "of no use"? You are a kind-hearted fellow, Johns. I am sure that if only you thought it over carefully you would consent to have them poisoned in some painless manner.'

Captain Sellers twitched his thin, sinuous lips.

'Make ghosts of them,' he suggested, pointedly.

At the mention of ghosts Captain Johns became shy, in his perplexed, sly, and unlovely manner.

Captain Ashton winked.

'Yes. And then perhaps you would get a chance to have a communication with the world of spirits. Surely the ghosts of seamen should haunt ships. Some of them would be sure to call on an old shipmate.'

Captain Sellers remarked drily:

'Don't raise his hopes like this. It's cruel. He won't see anything. You know, Johns, that nobody has ever seen a ghost.'

At this intolerable provocation Captain Johns came out of his reserve. With no perplexity whatever, but with a positive passion of credulity giving momentary lustre to his dull little eyes, he brought up a lot of authenticated instances. There were books and books full of instances. It was merest ignorance to deny supernatural apparitions. Cases were published every month in a special newspaper. Professor Cranks saw ghosts daily. And Professor Cranks was no small potatoes either. One of the biggest scientific men living. And there was that newspaper fellow – what's his name? – who had a girl-ghost visitor. He printed in his paper things she said to him. And to say there were no ghosts after that!

'Why, they have been photographed! What more proof do you want?'

Captain Johns was indignant. Captain Bell's lips twitched, but Captain Ashton protested now.

'For goodness' sake don't keep him going with that. And by the by, Johns, who's that hairy pirate you've got for your new mate? Nobody in the Dock seems to have seen him before.'

Captain Johns, pacified by the change of subjects, answered simply that Willy, the tobacconist at the corner of Fenchurch Street, had sent him along.

Willy, his shop, and the very house in Fenchurch Street, I believe, are gone now. In his time, wearing a careworn, absent-minded look on his pasty face, Willy served with tobacco many southern-going ships out of the Port of London. At certain times of the day the shop would be full of shipmasters. They sat on casks, they lounged against the counter.

Many a youngster found his first lift in life there; many a man got a sorely needed berth by simply dropping in for four pennyworth of birds'-eye at an auspicious moment. Even Willy's assistant, a redheaded, uninterested, delicate-looking young fellow, would hand you across the counter sometimes a bit of valuable intelligence with your box of cigarettes, in a whisper, lips hardly moving, thus, 'The *Bellona*, South Dock. Second officer wanted. You may be in time for it if you hurry up.'

And didn't one just fly!

'Oh, Willy sent him,' said Captain Ashton. 'He's a very striking man. If you were to put a red sash round his waist and a red handkerchief round his head he would look exactly like one of them buccaneering chaps that made men walk the plank and carried women off into captivity. Look out, Johns, he don't cut your throat for you and run off with the *Sapphire*. What ship has he come out of last?'

Captain Johns, after looking up credulously as usual, wrinkled his brow, and said placidly that the man had seen better days. His name was Bunter.

'He's had command of a Liverpool ship, the *Samaria*, some years ago. He lost her in the Indian Ocean, and had his certificate suspended for a year. Ever since then he has not been able to get another command. He's been knocking about in the Western Ocean trade lately.'

'That accounts for him being a stranger to everybody about the Docks,' Captain Ashton concluded as they rose from table.

Captain Johns walked down to the Dock after lunch. He was short of stature and slightly bandy. His appearance did not inspire the generality of mankind with esteem; but it must have been otherwise with his employers. He had the reputation of being an uncomfortable commander, meticulous in trifles, always nursing a grievance of some sort and incessantly nagging. He was not a man to kick up a row with you and be done with it, but to say nasty things in a whining voice; a man capable of making one's life a perfect misery if he took a dislike to an officer.

That very evening I went to see Bunter on board, and sympathised with him on his prospects for the voyage. He was subdued. I suppose a man with a secret locked up in his breast loses his buoyancy. And there was another reason why I could not expect Bunter to show a great elasticity of spirits. For one thing he had been very seedy lately, and besides – but of that later.

Captain Johns had been on board that afternoon and had loitered and dodged about his chief mate in a manner which had annoyed Bunter exceedingly.

'What could he mean?' he asked with calm exasperation. 'One would think he suspected I had stolen something and tried to see in what pocket I had stowed it away; or that somebody told him I had a tail and he wanted to find out how I managed to conceal it. I don't like to be approached from behind several times in one afternoon in that creepy way and then to be looked up at suddenly in front from under my elbow. Is it a new sort of peep-bo game? It doesn't amuse me. I am no longer a baby.'

I assured him that if anyone were to tell Captain Johns that he – Bunter – had a tail, Johns would manage to get himself to believe the story in some mysterious manner. He would. He was suspicious and credulous to an inconceivable degree. He would believe any silly tale, suspect any man of anything, and crawl about with it and ruminate the stuff, and turn it over and over in his mind in the most miserable, inwardly whining perplexity. He would take the meanest possible view in the end, and discover the meanest possible course of action by a sort of natural genius for that sort of thing.

Bunter also told me that the mean creature had crept all over the ship on his little, bandy legs, taking him along to grumble and whine to about a lot of trifles. Crept about the decks like a wretched insect – like a cockroach, only not so lively.

Thus did the self-possessed Bunter express himself with great disgust. Then, going on with his usual stately deliberation, made sinister by the frown of his jet black eyebrows:

'And the fellow is mad, too. He tried to be sociable for a bit, and could find nothing else but to make big eyes at me, and ask me if I believed "in communication beyond the grave." Communication beyond – I didn't know what he meant at first. I didn't know what to say. "A very solemn subject, Mr Bunter," says he. "I've given a great deal of study to it."'

Had Johns lived on shore he would have been the predestined prey of fraudulent mediums; or even if he had had any decent opportunities between the voyages. Luckily for him, when in England, he lived somewhere far away in Leytonstone, with a maiden sister ten years older than himself, a fearsome virago twice his size, before whom he trembled. It was said she bullied him terribly in general; and in the particular instance of his spiritualistic leanings she had her own views.

These leanings were to her simply satanic. She was reported as having declared that, 'With God's help, she would prevent that fool from giving himself up to the Devils.' It was beyond doubt that Johns's secret ambition was to get into personal communication with the spirits of the dead – if only his sister would let him. But she was adamant. I was told that while in London he had to account to her for every penny of the money he took with him in the morning, and for every hour of his time. And she kept the bankbook, too.

Bunter (he had been a wild youngster, but he was well connected; had ancestors; there was a family tomb somewhere in the home counties) – Bunter was indignant, perhaps on account of his own dead. Those steely blue eyes of his flashed with positive ferocity out of that black-bearded face. He impressed me – there was so much dark passion in his leisurely contempt.

'The cheek of the fellow! Enter into relations with... A mean little cad like this! It would be an impudent intrusion. He wants to enter!... What is it? A new sort of snobbishness or what?'

I laughed outright at this original view of spiritism – or whatever the ghost craze is called. Even Bunter himself condescended to smile. But it was an austere, quickly vanished smile. A man in his almost, I may say, tragic position couldn't be expected – you understand. He was really worried. He was ready eventually to put up with any dirty trick in the course of the voyage. A man could not expect much consideration should he find himself at the mercy of a fellow like Johns. A misfortune is a misfortune, and there's an end of it. But to be bored by mean, low-spirited, inane ghost stories in the Johns style, all the way out to Calcutta and back again, was an intolerable apprehension to be under. Spiritism was indeed a solemn subject to think about in that light. Dreadful, even!

Poor fellow! Little we both thought that before very long he himself... However, I could give him no comfort. I was rather appalled myself.

Bunter had also another annoyance that day. A confounded berthing master came on board on some pretence or other, but in reality, Bunter thought, simply impelled by an inconvenient curiosity – inconvenient to Bunter, that is. After some beating about the bush, that man suddenly said:

'I can't help thinking I've seen you before somewhere, Mr Mate. If I heard your name, perhaps Bunter – '

That's the worst of a life with a mystery in it – he was much alarmed. It was very likely that the man had seen him before – worse luck to his excellent memory. Bunter himself could not be expected to remember every casual dock walloper he might have had to do with. Bunter brazened it out by turning upon the man, making use of that impressive, black-as-night sternness of expression his unusual hair furnished him with:

'My name's Bunter, sir. Does that enlighten your inquisitive intellect? And I don't ask what your name may be. I don't want to know. I've no use for it, sir. An individual who calmly tells me to my face that he is *not sure* if he has seen me before, either means to be impudent or is no better than a worm, sir. Yes, I said a worm – a blind worm!'

Brave Bunter. That was the line to take. He fairly drove the beggar out of the ship, as if every word had been a blow. But the pertinacity of that brass-bound Paul Pry was astonishing. He cleared out of the ship, of course, before Bunter's ire, not saying anything, and only trying to cover up his retreat by a sickly smile. But once on the Jetty he turned deliberately round, and set himself to stare in dead earnest at the ship. He remained planted there like a mooring post, absolutely motionless, and with his stupid eyes winking no more than a pair of cabin portholes.

What could Bunter do? It was awkward for him, you know. He could not go and put his head into the bread locker. What he did was to take up a position abaft the mizzen rigging, and stare back as unwinking as the other. So they remained, and I don't know which of them grew giddy first; but the man on the Jetty, not having the advantage of something to hold on to, got tired the soonest, flung his arm, giving the contest up, as it were, and went away at last.

Bunter told me he was glad the *Sapphire*, 'that gem amongst ships' as he alluded to her sarcastically, was going to sea next day. He had had enough of the Dock. I understood his impatience. He had steeled himself against any possible worry the voyage might bring, though it is clear enough now that he was not prepared for the extraordinary experience that was awaiting him already, and in no other part of the world than the Indian Ocean itself; the very part of the world where the poor fellow had lost his ship and had broken his luck, as it seemed for good and all, at the same time.

As to his remorse in regard to a certain secret action of his life, well, I understand that a man of Bunter's fine character would suffer not a little. Still, between ourselves, and without the slightest wish to be cynical, it cannot be denied that with the noblest of us the fear of being found out enters for some considerable part into the composition of remorse. I didn't say this in so many words to Bunter, but, as the poor fellow harped a bit on it, I told him that there were skeletons in a good many honest cupboards, and that, as to his own particular guilt, it wasn't writ large on his face for everybody to see – so he needn't worry as to that. And besides, he would be gone to sea in about twelve hours from now.

He said there was some comfort in that thought, and went off then to spend his last evening for many months with his wife. For all his wildness, Bunter had made no mistake in his marrying. He had married a lady. A perfect lady. She was a dear little woman, too. As to her pluck, I, who know what times they had to go through, I cannot admire her enough for it. Real, hard-wearing every day and day after day pluck that only a woman is capable of when she is of the right sort – the undismayed sort I would call it.

The black mate felt this parting with his wife more than any of the previous ones in all the years of bad luck. But she was of the undismayed kind, and showed less trouble in her gentle face than the black-haired, buccaneer-like, but dignified mate of the *Sapphire*. It may be that her conscience was less disturbed than her husband's. Of course, his life had no secret places for her; but a woman's conscience is somewhat more resourceful in finding good and valid excuses. It depends greatly on the person that needs them, too.

They had agreed that she should not come down to the Dock to see him off. 'I wonder you care to look at me at all,' said the sensitive man. And she did not laugh.

Bunter was very sensitive; he left her rather brusquely at the last. He got on board in good time, and produced the usual impression on the mud pilot in the broken-down straw hat who took the *Sapphire* out of dock. The river man was very polite to the dignified, striking-looking chief mate. 'The five inch manilla for the check rope, Mr – Bunter, thank you – Mr Bunter, please.' The sea pilot who left the 'gem of ships' heading comfortably down Channel off Dover told some of his friends that, this voyage, the *Sapphire* had for chief mate a man who seemed a jolly sight too good for old Johns. 'Bunter's his name. I wonder where he's sprung from? Never seen him before in any ship I piloted in or out all these years. He's the sort of man you don't forget. You couldn't. A thorough good sailor, too. And won't old Johns just worry his head off! Unless the old fool should take fright at him – for he does not seem the sort of man that would let himself be put upon without letting you know what he thinks of you. And that's exactly what old Johns would be more afraid of than of anything else.'

As this is really meant to be the record of a spiritualistic experience which came, if not precisely to Captain Johns himself, at any rate to his ship, there is no use in recording the other events of the passage out. It was an ordinary passage, the crew was an ordinary crew, the weather was of the usual kind. The black mate's quiet, sedate method of going to work had given a sober tone to the life of the ship. Even in gales of wind everything went on quietly somehow.

There was only one severe blow which made things fairly lively for all hands for full four-and-twenty hours. That was off the coast of Africa, after passing the Cape of Good Hope. At the very height of it several heavy seas were shipped with no serious results, but there was a considerable smashing of breakable objects in the pantry and in the staterooms. Mr Bunter, who was so greatly respected on board, found himself treated scurvily by the Southern Ocean, which, bursting open the door of his room like a ruffianly burglar, carried off several useful things, and made all the others extremely wet.

Later, on the same day, the Southern Ocean caused the *Sapphire* to lurch over in such an unrestrained fashion that the two drawers fitted under Mr Bunter's sleeping berth flew out altogether, spilling all their contents. They ought, of course, to have been locked, and Mr Bunter had only to thank himself for what had happened. He ought to have turned the key on each before going out on deck.

His consternation was very great. The steward, who was paddling about all the time with swabs, trying to dry out the flooded cuddy, heard him exclaim, 'Hallo!' in a startled and dismayed tone. In the midst of his work the steward felt a sympathetic concern for the mate's distress.

Captain Johns was secretly glad when he heard of the damage. He was indeed afraid of his chief mate, as the sea pilot had ventured to foretell, and afraid of him for the very reason the sea pilot had put forward as likely.

Captain Johns, therefore, would have liked very much to hold that black mate of his at his mercy in some way or other. But the man was irreproachable, as near absolute perfection as could be. And Captain Johns was much annoyed, and at the same time congratulated himself on his chief officer's efficiency.

He made a great show of living sociably with him, on the principle that the more friendly you are with a man the more easily you may catch him tripping; and also for the reason that he wanted to have somebody who would listen to his stories of manifestations, apparitions, ghosts, and all the rest of the imbecile spook lore. He had it all at his fingers' ends; and he spun those ghostly yarns in a persistent, colourless voice, giving them a futile turn peculiarly his own.

'I like to converse with my officers,' he used to say. 'There are masters that hardly ever open their mouths from beginning to end of a passage for fear of losing their dignity. What's that, after all – this bit of position a man holds!'

His sociability was most to be dreaded in the second dog watch, because he was one of those men who grow lively towards the evening, and the officer on duty was unable then to find excuses for leaving the poop. Captain Johns would pop up the companion suddenly, and, sidling up in his creeping way to poor Bunter, as he walked up and down, would fire into him some spiritualistic proposition, such as:

'Spirits, male and female, show a good deal of refinement in a general way, don't they?'

To which Bunter, holding his black-whiskered head high, would mutter:

'I don't know.'

'Ah! That's because you don't want to. You are the most obstinate, prejudiced man I've ever met, Mr Bunter. I told you you may have any book out of my bookcase. You may just go into my stateroom and help yourself to any volume.'

And if Bunter protested that he was too tired in his watches below to spare any time for reading, Captain Johns would smile nastily behind his back, and remark that of course some people needed more sleep than others to keep themselves fit for their work. If Mr Bunter was afraid of not keeping properly awake when on duty at night, that was another matter.

'But I think you borrowed a novel to read from the second mate the other day – a trashy pack of lies,' Captain Johns sighed. 'I am afraid you are not a spiritually minded man, Mr Bunter. That's what's the matter.'

Sometimes he would appear on deck in the middle of the night, looking very grotesque and bandy-legged in his sleeping suit. At that sight the persecuted Bunter would wring his hands stealthily, and break out into moisture all over his forehead. After standing sleepily by the binnacle, scratching himself in an unpleasant manner, Captain Johns was sure to start on some aspect or other of his only topic.

He would, for instance, discourse on the improvement of morality to be expected from the establishment of general and close intercourse with the spirits of the departed. The spirits, Captain Johns thought, would consent to associate familiarly with the living if it were not for the unbelief of the great mass of mankind. He himself would not care to have anything to do with a crowd that would not believe in his – Captain Johns's – existence. Then why should a spirit? This was asking too much.

He went on breathing hard by the binnacle and trying to reach round his shoulder blades; then, with a thick, drowsy severity, declared:

'Incredulity, sir, is the evil of the age!'

It rejected the evidence of Professor Cranks and of the journalist chap. It resisted the production of photographs.

For Captain Johns believed firmly that certain spirits had been photographed. He had read something of it in the papers. And the idea of it having been done had got a tremendous hold on him, because his mind was not critical. Bunter said afterwards that nothing could be more weird than this little man, swathed in a sleeping suit three sizes too large for him, shuffling with excitement in the moonlight near the wheel, and shaking his fist at the serene sea.

'Photographs! photographs!' he would repeat, in a voice as creaky as a rusty hinge.

The very helmsman just behind him got uneasy at that performance, not being capable of understanding exactly what the 'old man was kicking up a row with the mate about.'

Then Johns, after calming down a bit, would begin again.

'The sensitised plate can't lie. No, sir.'

Nothing could be more funny than this ridiculous little man's conviction – his dogmatic tone. Bunter would go on swinging up and down the poop like a deliberate, dignified pendulum. He said not a word. But the poor fellow had not a trifle on his conscience, as you know; and to have imbecile ghosts rammed down his throat like this on top of his own worry nearly drove him crazy. He knew that on many occasions he was on the verge of lunacy, because he could not help indulging in half-delirious visions of Captain Johns being picked up by the scruff of the neck and dropped over the taffrail into the ship's wake – the sort of thing no sane sailorman would think of doing to a cat or any other animal, anyhow. He imagined him bobbing up – a tiny black speck left far astern on the moonlit ocean.

I don't think that even at the worst moments Bunter really desired to drown Captain Johns. I fancy that all his disordered imagination longed for was merely to stop the ghostly inanity of the skipper's talk.

But, all the same, it was a dangerous form of self-indulgence. Just picture to yourself that ship in the Indian Ocean, on a clear, tropical night, with her sails full and still, the watch on deck stowed away out of sight; and on her poop, flooded with moonlight, the stately black mate walking up and down with measured, dignified steps, preserving an awful silence, and that grotesquely mean little figure in striped flannelette alternately creaking and droning of 'personal intercourse beyond the grave.'

It makes me creepy all over to think of. And sometimes the folly of Captain Johns would appear clothed in a sort of weird utilitarianism. How useful it would be if the spirits of the departed could be induced to take a practical interest in the affairs of the living! What a help, say, to the police, for instance, in the detection of crime! The number of murders, at any rate, would be considerably reduced, he guessed with an air of great sagacity. Then he would give way to grotesque discouragement.

Where was the use of trying to communicate with people that had no faith, and more likely than not would scorn the offered information? Spirits had their feelings. They were *all* feelings in a way. But he was surprised at the forbearance shown towards murderers by their victims. That was the sort of apparition that no guilty man would dare to pooh-pooh. And perhaps the undiscovered murderers – whether believing or not – were haunted. They wouldn't be likely to boast about it, would they?

'For myself,' he pursued, in a sort of vindictive, malevolent whine, 'if anybody murdered me I would not let him forget it. I would wither him up – I would terrify him to death.'

The idea of his skipper's ghost terrifying anyone was so ludicrous that the black mate, little disposed to mirth as he was, could not help giving vent to a weary laugh.

And this laugh, the only acknowledgment of a long and earnest discourse, offended Captain Johns.

'What's there to laugh at in this conceited manner, Mr Bunter?' he snarled. 'Supernatural visitations have terrified better men than you. Don't you allow me enough soul to make a ghost of?'

I think it was the nasty tone that caused Bunter to stop short and turn about.

'I shouldn't wonder,' went on the angry fanatic of spiritism, 'if you weren't one of them people that take no more account of a man than if he were a beast. You would be capable, I don't doubt, to deny the possession of an immortal soul to your own father.'

And then Bunter, being bored beyond endurance, and also exasperated by the private worry, lost his self-possession.

He walked up suddenly to Captain Johns, and, stooping a little to look close into his face, said, in a low, even tone:

'You don't know what a man like me is capable of.'

Captain Johns threw his head back, but was too astonished to budge. Bunter resumed his walk; and for a long time his measured footsteps and the low wash of the water alongside were the only sounds which troubled the silence brooding over the great waters. Then Captain Johns cleared his throat uneasily, and, after sidling away towards the companion for greater safety, plucked up enough courage to retreat under an act of authority:

'Raise the starboard clew of the mainsail, and lay the yards dead square, Mr Bunter. Don't you see the wind is nearly right aft?'

Bunter at once answered 'Ay, ay, sir,' though there was not the slightest necessity to touch the yards, and the wind was well out on the quarter. While he was executing the order Captain Johns hung on the companion steps, growling to himself, 'Walk this poop like an admiral and don't even notice when the yards want trimming!' – loud enough for the helmsman to overhear. Then he sank slowly backwards out of the man's sight; and when he reached the bottom of the stairs he stood still and thought.

'He's an awful ruffian, with all his gentlemanly airs. No more gentleman mates for me.'

Two nights afterwards he was slumbering peacefully in his berth, when a heavy thumping just above his head (a well-understood signal that he was wanted on deck) made him leap out of bed, broad awake in a moment.

'What's up?' he muttered, running out barefooted. On passing through the cabin he glanced at the clock. It was the middle watch. 'What on earth can the mate want me for?' he thought.

Bolting out of the companion, he found a clear, dewy moonlit night and a strong, steady breeze. He looked around wildly. There was no one on the poop except the helmsman, who addressed him at once.

'It was me, sir. I let go the wheel for a second to stamp over your head. I am afraid there's something wrong with the mate.'

'Where's he got to?' asked the captain sharply.

The man, who was obviously nervous, said:

'The last I saw of him was as he fell down the port poopladder.'

'Fell down the poop-ladder! What did he do that for? What made him?'

'I don't know, sir. He was walking the port side. Then just as he turned towards me to come aft...'

'You saw him?' interrupted the captain.

'I did. I was looking at him. And I heard the crash, too – something awful. Like the mainmast going overboard. It was as if something had struck him.'

Captain Johns became very uneasy and alarmed. 'Come,' he said sharply. 'Did anybody strike him? What did you see?'

'Nothing, sir, so help me! There was nothing to see. He just gave a little sort of hallo! threw his hands before him, and over he went – crash. I couldn't hear anything more, so I just let go the wheel for a second to call you up.'

'You're scared!' said Captain Johns.

'I am, sir, straight!'

Captain Johns stared at him. The silence of his ship driving on her way seemed to contain a danger – a mystery. He was reluctant to go and look for his mate himself, in the shadows of the main deck, so quiet, so still.

All he did was to advance to the break of the poop, and call for the watch. As the sleepy men came trooping aft, he shouted to them fiercely:

'Look at the foot of the port poop-ladder, some of you! See the mate lying there?'

Their startled exclamations told him immediately that they did see him. Somebody even screeched out emotionally, 'He's dead!'

Mr Bunter was laid in his bunk and when the lamp in his room was lit he looked indeed as if he were dead, but it was obvious also that he was breathing yet. The steward had been roused out, the second mate called and sent on deck to look after the ship, and for an hour or so Captain Johns devoted himself silently to the restoring of consciousness. Mr Bunter at last opened his eyes, but he could not speak. He was dazed and inert. The steward bandaged a nasty scalp wound while Captain Johns held an additional light. They had to cut away a lot of Mr Bunter's jet black hair to make a good dressing. This done, and after gazing for a while at their patient, the two left the cabin.

'A rum go, this, steward,' said Captain Johns in the passage.

'Yessir.'

'A sober man that's right in his head does not fall down a poop-ladder like a sack of potatoes. The ship's as steady as a church.'

'Yessir. Fit of some kind, I shouldn't wonder.'

'Well, I should. He doesn't look as if he were subject to fits and giddiness. Why, the man's in the prime of life. I wouldn't have another kind of mate – not if I knew it. You don't think he has a private store of liquor, do you, eh? He seemed to me a bit strange in his manner several times lately. Off his feed, too, a bit, I noticed.'

'Well, sir, if he ever had a bottle or two of grog in his cabin, that must have gone a long time ago. I saw him throw some broken glass overboard after the last gale we had; but that didn't amount to anything. Anyway, sir, you couldn't call Mr Bunter a drinking man.'

'No,' conceded the captain, reflectively. And the steward, locking the pantry door, tried to escape out of the passage, thinking he could manage to snatch another hour of sleep before it was time for him to turn out for the day.

Captain Johns shook his head.

'There's some mystery there.'

'There's special Providence that he didn't crack his head like an eggshell on the quarterdeck mooring-bits, sir. The men tell me he couldn't have missed them by more than an inch.'

And the steward vanished skilfully.

Captain Johns spent the rest of the night and the whole of the ensuing day between his own room and that of the mate.

In his own room he sat with his open hands reposing on his knees, his lips pursed up, and the horizontal furrows on his forehead marked very heavily. Now and then raising his arm by a slow, as if cautious movement, he scratched lightly the top of his bald head. In the mate's room he stood for long periods of time with his hand to his lips, gazing at the half-conscious man.

For three days Mr Bunter did not say a single word. He looked at people sensibly enough but did not seem to be able to hear any questions put to him. They cut off some more of his hair and swathed his head in wet cloths. He took some nourishment, and was made as comfortable as possible. At dinner on the third day the second mate remarked to the captain, in connection with the affair:

'These half-round brass plates on the steps of the poop-ladders are beastly dangerous things!'

'Are they?' retorted Captain Johns, sourly. 'It takes more than a brass plate to account for an able-bodied man crashing down in this fashion like a felled ox.'

The second mate was impressed by that view. There was something in that, he thought.

'And the weather fine, everything dry, and the ship going along as steady as a church!' pursued Captain Johns, gruffly.

As Captain Johns continued to look extremely sour, the second mate did not open his lips any more during the dinner. Captain Johns was annoyed and hurt by an innocent remark, because the fitting of the aforesaid brass plates had been done at his suggestion only the voyage before, in order to smarten up the appearance of the poop-ladders.

On the fourth day Mr Bunter looked decidedly better; very languid yet, of course, but he heard and understood what was said to him, and even could say a few words in a feeble voice.

Captain Johns, coming in, contemplated him attentively, without much visible sympathy.

'Well, can you give us your account of this accident, Mr Bunter?'

Bunter moved slightly his bandaged head, and fixed his cold blue stare on Captain Johns's face, as if taking stock and appraising the value of every feature; the perplexed forehead, the credulous eyes, the inane droop of the mouth. And he gazed so long that Captain Johns grew restive, and looked over his shoulder at the door.

'No accident,' breathed out Bunter, in a peculiar tone.

'You don't mean to say you've got the falling sickness,' said Captain Johns. 'How would you call it signing as chief mate of a clipper ship with a thing like that on you?'

Bunter answered him only by a sinister look. The skipper shuffled his feet a little.

'Well, what made you have that tumble, then?'

Bunter raised himself a little, and, looking straight into Captain Johns's eyes said, in a very distinct whisper:

'You – were – right!'

He fell back and closed his eyes. Not a word more could Captain Johns get out of him; and, the steward coming into the cabin, the skipper withdrew.

But that very night, unobserved, Captain Johns, opening the door cautiously, entered again the mate's cabin. He could wait no longer. The suppressed eagerness, the excitement expressed in all his mean, creeping little person, did not escape the chief mate, who was lying awake, looking frightfully pulled down and perfectly impassive.

'You are coming to gloat over me, I suppose,' said Bunter without moving, and yet making a palpable hit.

'Bless my soul!' exclaimed Captain Johns with a start, and assuming a sobered demeanour. 'There's a thing to say!'

'Well, gloat, then! You and your ghosts, you've managed to get over a live man.'

This was said by Bunter without stirring, in a low voice, and with not much expression.

'Do you mean to say,' inquired Captain Johns, in awe-struck whisper, 'that you had a supernatural experience that night? You saw an apparition, then, on board my ship?'

Reluctance, shame, disgust, would have been visible on poor Bunter's countenance if the great part of it had not been swathed up in cotton wool and bandages. His ebony eyebrows, more sinister than ever amongst all that lot of white linen, came together in a frown as he made a mighty effort to say:

'Yes, I have seen.'

The wretchedness in his eyes would have awakened the compassion of any other man than Captain Johns. But Captain Johns was all agog with triumphant excitement. He was just a little bit frightened, too. He looked at that unbelieving scoffer laid low, and did not even dimly guess at his profound, humiliating distress. He was not generally capable of taking much part in the anguish of his fellow creatures. This time, moreover, he was excessively anxious to know what had happened. Fixing his credulous eyes on the bandaged head, he asked, trembling slightly:

'And did it – did it knock you down?'

'Come! am I the sort of man to be knocked down by a ghost?' protested Bunter in a little stronger tone. 'Don't you remember what you said yourself the other night? Better men than me – Ha! You'll have to look a long time before you find a better man for a mate of your ship.'

Captain Johns pointed a solemn finger at Bunter's bedplace.

'You've been terrified,' he said. 'That's what's the matter. You've been terrified. Why, even the man at the wheel was scared, though he couldn't see anything. He *felt* the supernatural. You are punished for your incredulity, Mr Bunter. You were terrified.'

'And suppose I was,' said Bunter. 'Do you know what I had seen? Can you conceive the sort of ghost that would haunt a man like me? Do you think it was a ladyish, afternoon call, another-cup-of-tea-please apparition that visits your Professor Cranks and that journalist chap you are always talking about? No; I can't tell you what it was like. Every man has his own ghosts. You couldn't conceive...'

Bunter stopped, out of breath; and Captain Johns remarked, with the glow of inward satisfaction reflected in his tone:

'I've always thought you were the sort of man that was ready for anything; from pitch-and-toss to wilful murder, as the saying goes. Well, well! So you were terrified.'

'I stepped back,' said Bunter, curtly. 'I don't remember anything else.'

'The man at the wheel told me you went backwards as if something had hit you.'

'It was a sort of inward blow,' explained Bunter. 'Something too deep for you, Captain Johns, to understand. Your life and mine haven't been the same. Aren't you satisfied to see me converted?'

'And you can't tell me any more?' asked Captain Johns, anxiously.

'No, I can't. I wouldn't. It would be no use if I did. That sort of experience must be gone through. Say I am being punished. Well, I take my punishment, but talk of it I won't.'

'Very well,' said Captain Johns; 'you won't. But, mind, I can draw my own conclusions from that.'

'Draw what you like; but be careful what you say, sir. You don't terrify me. *You* aren't a ghost.'

'One word. Has it any connection with what you said to me on that last night, when we had a talk together on spiritualism?'

Bunter looked weary and puzzled.

'What did I say?'

'You told me that I couldn't know what a man like you was capable of.'

'Yes, yes. Enough!'

'Very good. I am fixed, then,' remarked Captain Johns. 'All I say is that I am jolly glad not to be you, though I would have given almost anything for the privilege of personal communication with the world of spirits. Yes, sir, but not in that way.'

Poor Bunter moaned pitifully.

'It has made me feel twenty years older.'

Captain Johns retired quietly. He was delighted to observe this overbearing ruffian humbled to the dust by the moralising agency of the spirits. The whole occurrence was a source of pride and gratification; and he began to feel a sort of regard for his chief mate.

It is true that in further interviews Bunter showed himself very mild and deferential. He seemed to cling to his captain for spiritual protection. He used to send for him, and say, 'I feel so nervous,' and Captain Johns would stay patiently for hours in the hot little cabin, and feel proud of the call.

For Mr Bunter was ill, and could not leave his berth for a good many days. He became a convinced spiritualist, not enthusiastically – that could hardly have been expected from him – but in a grim, unshakeable way. He could not be called exactly friendly to the disembodied inhabitants of our globe, as Captain Johns was. But he was now a firm, if gloomy, recruit of spiritualism.

One afternoon, as the ship was already well to the north in the Gulf of Bengal, the steward knocked at the door of the captain's cabin, and said, without opening it:

'The mate asks if you could spare him a moment, sir. He seems to be in a state in there.'

Captain Johns jumped up from the couch at once.

'Yes. Tell him I am coming.'

He thought: Could it be possible there had been another spiritual manifestation – in the daytime, too!

He revelled in the hope. It was not exactly that, however. Still, Bunter, whom he saw sitting collapsed in a chair – he had been up for several days, but not on deck as yet – poor Bunter had something startling enough to communicate. His hands covered his face. His legs were stretched straight out, dismally.

'What's the news now?' croaked Captain Johns, not unkindly, because in truth it always pleased him to see Bunter – as he expressed it – tamed.

'News!' exclaimed the crushed sceptic through his hands. 'Ay, news enough, Captain Johns. Who will be able to deny the awfulness, the genuineness? Another man would have dropped dead. You want to know what I had seen. All I can tell you is that since I've seen it my hair is turning white.'

Bunter detached his hands from his face, and they hung on each side of his chair as if dead. He looked broken in the dusky cabin.

'You don't say!' stammered out Captain Johns. 'Turned white! Hold on a bit! I'll light the lamp!'

When the lamp was lit, the startling phenomenon could be seen plainly enough. As if the dread, the horror, the anguish of the supernatural were being exhaled through the pores of his skin, a sort of silvery mist seemed to cling to the cheeks and the head of the mate. His short beard, his cropped hair, were growing, not black, but grey – almost white.

When Mr Bunter, thin-faced and shaky, came on deck for duty, he was clean-shaven, and his head was white. The hands were awe-struck. 'Another man,' they whispered to each other. It was generally and mysteriously agreed that the mate had 'seen something,' with the exception of the man at the wheel at the time, who maintained that the mate was 'struck by something.'

This distinction hardly amounted to a difference. On the other hand, everybody admitted that, after he picked up his strength a bit, he seemed even smarter in his movements than before.

One day in Calcutta, Captain Johns, pointing out to a visitor his white-headed chief mate standing by the main hatch, was heard to say oracularly:

'That man's in the prime of life.'

Of course, while Bunter was away, I called regularly on Mrs Bunter every Saturday, just to see whether she had any use for my services. It was understood I would do that. She had just his half-pay to live on – it amounted to about a pound a week. She had taken one room in a quiet little square in the East End.

And this was affluence to what I had heard that the couple were reduced to for a time after Bunter had to give up the Western Ocean trade – he used to go as mate of all sorts of hard packets after he lost his ship and his luck together – it was affluence to that time when Bunter would start at seven o'clock in the morning with but a glass of hot water and a crust of dry bread. It won't stand thinking about, especially for those who know Mrs Bunter. I had seen something of them, too, at that time; and it just makes me shudder to remember what that born lady had to put up with. Enough!

Dear Mrs Bunter used to worry a good deal after the *Sapphire* left for Calcutta. She would say to me, 'It must be so awful for poor Winston' – Winston is Bunter's name – and I tried to comfort her the best I could. Afterwards, she got some small children to teach in a family, and was half the day with them, and the occupation was good for her.

In the very first letter she had from Calcutta, Bunter told her he had had a fall down the poop-ladder, and cut his head, but no bones broken, thank God. That was all. Of course, she had other letters from him, but that vagabond Bunter never gave me a scratch of the pen the solid eleven months. I supposed, naturally, that everything was going on all right. Who could imagine what was happening?

Then one day dear Mrs Bunter got a letter from a legal firm in the City, advising her that her uncle was dead – her old curmudgeon of an uncle – a retired stockbroker, a heartless, petrified antiquity that had lasted on and on. He was nearly ninety, I believe; and if I were to meet his venerable ghost this minute, I would try to take him by the throat and strangle him.

The old beast would never forgive his niece for marrying Bunter; and years afterwards, when people made a point of letting him know that she was in London, pretty nearly starving at forty years of age, he only said, 'Serve the little fool right!' I believe he meant her to starve. And, lo and behold, the old cannibal died intestate, with no other relatives but that very identical little fool. The Bunters were wealthy people now.

Of course, Mrs Bunter wept as if her heart would break. In any other woman it would have been mere hypocrisy. Naturally, too, she wanted to cable the news to her Winston in Calcutta, but I showed her, *Gazette* in hand, that the ship was on the homeward-bound list for more than a week already. So we sat down to wait, and talked meantime of dear old Winston every day. There were just one hundred such days before the *Sapphire* got reported 'All well' in the chops of the Channel by an incoming mailboat.

'I am going to Dunkirk to meet him,' says she. The *Sapphire* had a cargo of jute for Dunkirk. Of course, I had to escort the dear lady in the quality of her 'ingenious friend.' She calls me 'our ingenious friend' to this day; and I've observed some people – strangers – looking hard at me, for the signs of the ingenuity, I suppose.

After settling Mrs Bunter in a good hotel in Dunkirk, I walked down to the docks – late afternoon it was – and what was my surprise to see the ship actually fast alongside. Either

Johns or Bunter, or both, must have been driving her hard up Channel. Anyway, she had been in since the day before last, and her crew was already paid off. I met two of her apprenticed boys going off home on leave with their dunnage on a Frenchman's barrow, as happy as larks, and I asked them if the mate was on board.

'There he is, on the quay, looking at the moorings,' says one of the youngsters as he skipped past me.

You may imagine the shock to my feelings when I beheld his white head. I could only manage to tell him that his wife was at an hotel in town. He left me at once, to go and get his hat on board. I was mightily surprised by the smartness of his movements as he hurried up the gangway.

Whereas the black mate struck people as deliberate, and strangely stately in his gait for a man in the prime of life, this white-headed chap seemed the most wonderfully alert of old men. I don't suppose Bunter was any quicker on his pins than before. It was the colour of the hair that made all the difference in one's judgment.

The same with his eyes. Those eyes, that looked at you so steely, so fierce, and so fascinating out of a bush of a buccaneer's black hair, now had an innocent almost boyish expression in their good-humoured brightness under those white eyebrows.

I led him without any delay into Mrs Bunter's private sitting room. After she had dropped a tear over the late cannibal, given a hug to her Winston, and told him that he must grow his moustache again, the dear lady tucked her feet upon the sofa, and I got out of Bunter's way.

He started at once to pace the room, waving his long arms. He worked himself into a regular frenzy, and tore Johns limb from limb many times over that evening.

'Fell down? Of course I fell down, by slipping backwards on that fool's patent brass plates. 'Pon my word, I had been walking that poop in charge of the ship, and I didn't know whether I was in the Indian Ocean or in the moon. I was crazy. My head spun round and round with sheer worry. I had made my last application of your chemist's wonderful stuff.' (This to me.) 'All the store of bottles you gave me got smashed when those drawers fell out in the last gale. I had been getting some dry things to change, when I heard the cry, "All hands on deck!" and made one jump of it, without even pushing them in properly. Ass! When I came back and saw the broken glass and the mess, I felt ready to faint.

'No; look here – deception is bad; but not to be able to keep it up after one has been forced into it. You know that since I've been squeezed out of the Western Ocean packets by younger men, just on account of my grizzled muzzle – you know how much chance I had to ever get a ship. And not a soul to turn to. We have been a lonely couple, we two – she threw away everything for me – and to see her want a piece of dry bread – '

He banged with his fist fit to split the Frenchman's table in two.

'I would have turned a sanguinary pirate for her, let alone cheating my way into a berth by dyeing my hair. So when you came to me with your chemist's wonderful stuff – '

He checked himself.

'By the way, that fellow's got a fortune when he likes to pick it up. It is a wonderful stuff – you tell him salt water can do nothing to it. It stays on as long as your hair will.'

'All right,' I said. 'Go on.'

Thereupon he went for Johns again with a fury that frightened his wife, and made me laugh till I cried.

'Just you try to think what it would have meant to be at the mercy of the meanest creature that ever commanded a ship! Just fancy what a life that crawling Johns would have led me! And I knew that in a week or so the white hair would begin to show.

And the crew. Did you ever think of that? To be shown up as a low fraud before all hands. What a life for me till we got to Calcutta! And once there – kicked out, of course. Half-pay stopped. Annie here alone without a penny – starving; and I on the other side of the earth, ditto. You see?

'I thought of shaving twice a day. But could I shave my head, too? No way – no way at all. Unless I dropped Johns overboard; and even then –

'Do you wonder now that with all these things boiling in my head I didn't know where I was putting down my foot that night? I just felt myself falling – then crash, and all dark.

'When I came to myself that bang on the head seemed to have steadied my wits somehow. I was so sick of everything that for two days I wouldn't speak to anyone. They thought it was a slight concussion of the brain. Then the idea dawned upon me as I was looking at that ghost-ridden, wretched fool. "Ah, you love ghosts," I thought. "Well, you shall have something from beyond the grave."

'I didn't even trouble to invent a story. I couldn't imagine a ghost if I wanted to. I wasn't fit to lie connectedly if I had tried. I just bulled him on to it. Do you know, he got, quite by himself, a notion that at some time or other I had done somebody to death in some way, and that –'

'Oh, the horrible man!' cried Mrs Bunter from the sofa. There was a silence.

'And didn't he bore my head off on the home passage!' began Bunter again in a weary voice. 'He loved me. He was proud of me. I was converted. I had had a manifestation. Do you know what he was after? He wanted me and him "to make a *seance*," in his own words, and to try to call up that ghost (the one that had turned my hair white – the ghost of my supposed victim), and, as he said, talk it over with him – the ghost – in a friendly way.

'"Or else, Bunter," he says, "you may get another manifestation when you least expect it, and tumble overboard perhaps, or something. You ain't really safe till we pacify the spirit world in some way."

'Can you conceive a lunatic like that? No – say?'

I said nothing. But Mrs Bunter did, in a very decided tone.

'Winston, I don't want you to go on board that ship again any more.'

'My dear,' says he, 'I have all my things on board yet.'

'You don't want the things. Don't go near that ship at all.'

He stood still; then, dropping his eyes with a faint smile, said slowly, in a dreamy voice:

'The haunted ship.'

'And your last,' I added.

We carried him off, as he stood, by the night train. He was very quiet; but crossing the Channel, as we two had a smoke on deck, he turned to me suddenly, and, grinding his teeth, whispered:

'He'll never know how near he was being dropped overboard!'

He meant Captain Johns. I said nothing.

But Captain Johns, I understand, made a great to-do about the disappearance of his chief mate. He set the French police scouring the country for the body. In the end, I fancy he got word from his owners' office to drop all this fuss – that it was all right. I don't suppose he ever understood anything of that mysterious occurrence.

To this day he tries at times (he's retired now, and his conversation is not very coherent) – he tries to tell the story of a black mate he once had, 'a murderous, gentlemanly ruffian, with raven black hair which turned white all at once in consequence of a manifestation from beyond the grave.' An avenging apparition. What with reference to black and white hair, to poop-ladders, and to his own feelings and views, it is difficult to make head or tail of it. If his sister (she's very vigorous still) should be present she cuts all this short – peremptorily:

'Don't you mind what he says. He's got devils on the brain.'

Biographical note

Joseph Conrad was born Józef Teodor Konrad Korzeniowski to Polish parents in Berdichev in the Ukraine in 1857. His father, a landless gentleman, poet, and translator of English, French and German literature, was active in the Polish patriotic underground, which resulted in his imprisonment and his family's exile to Volagda in northern Russia and later in the eastern Ukraine. There, in Chernihiv, Conrad's mother died in 1867. Once released from exile, his father soon died of tuberculosis, and, from 1869, Conrad was supported by his uncle, Tadeusz Bobrowski. After school in Kraków, Conrad persuaded Bobrowski to let him join the French merchant marine with whom he was to travel to the West Indies several times between 1875 and 1878. His career continued in the British merchant marine, where he rose from common seaman to first mate, obtaining his master mariner's certificate, and, in 1886, command of his own vessel, *Otago*. (It was also in 1886, that Conrad became a British subject.) His following years at sea were to prove vastly influential on his writing, as he sailed all over the world, and, most famously, up the Congo river in 1890, a journey depicted in his tale, *Heart of Darkness* (written 1899, published 1902).

Conrad settled in England in 1894, and married Jessie George in 1896, having published his first novel, *Almayer's Folly*, in 1895. Writing in English, a language he did not learn until he was twenty, Conrad achieved belated financial and popular success with his late novel *Chance* (1913), although earlier works such as *Nostromo* (1904), *The Secret Agent* (1904), and *Under Western Eyes* (1911) are now held in greater critical esteem. Conrad died in 1924. After a brief period of neglect, he was declared by F.R. Leavis in 1941 as 'among the very greatest novelists in the language'.

HESPERUS PRESS

Hesperus Press, as suggested by the Latin motto, is committed to bringing near what is far – far both in space and time. Works written by the greatest authors, and unjustly neglected or simply little known in the English-speaking world, are made accessible through new translations and a completely fresh editorial approach. Through these classic works, the reader is introduced to the greatest writers from all times and all cultures.

For more information on Hesperus Press, please visit our website: **www.hesperuspress.com**

ET REMOTISSIMA PROPE

MODERN VOICES

SELECTED TITLES FROM HESPERUS PRESS

Author	Title	Foreword writer
Mikhail Bulgakov	*A Dog's Heart*	A.S. Byatt
Mikhail Bulgakov	*The Fatal Eggs*	Doris Lessing
Anthony Burgess	*The Eve of St Venus*	
Colette	*Claudine's House*	Doris Lessing
Marie Ferranti	*The Princess of Mantua*	
Beppe Fenoglio	*A Private Affair*	Paul Bailey
F. Scott Fitzgerald	*The Popular Girl*	Helen Dunmore
F. Scott Fitzgerald	*The Rich Boy*	John Updike
Graham Greene	*No Man's Land*	David Lodge
Franz Kafka	*Metamorphosis*	Martin Jarvis
Franz Kafka	*The Trial*	Zadie Smith
D.H. Lawrence	*Wintry Peacock*	Amit Chaudhuri
Rosamond Lehmann	*The Gipsy's Baby*	Niall Griffiths
Carlo Levi	*Words are Stones*	Anita Desai
André Malraux	*The Way of the Kings*	Rachel Seiffert
Katherine Mansfield	*In a German Pension*	Linda Grant
Katherine Mansfield	*Prelude*	William Boyd
Vladimir Mayakovsky	*My Discovery of America*	Colum McCann
Luigi Pirandello	*Loveless Love*	
Françoise Sagan	*The Unmade Bed*	
Jean-Paul Sartre	*The Wall*	Justin Cartwright
Bernard Shaw	*The Adventures of the Black Girl in Her Search for God*	Colm Tóibín
Georges Simenon	*Three Crimes*	
Leonard Woolf	*A Tale Told by Moonlight*	Victoria Glendinning
Virginia Woolf	*Memoirs of a Novelist*	

CET OUVRAGE
A ÉTÉ ACHEVÉ D'IMPRIMER
EN AOÛT 1995
SUR LES PRESSES DE L'IMPRIMERIE AGMV

CAP-SAINT-IGNACE (QUÉBEC)

POUR LE COMPTE
DE LEMÉAC ÉDITEUR

DÉPÔT LÉGAL
1re ÉDITION : 4e TRIMESTRE 1981
(ED 01/IMP 02)